THE ASTERISK WAR

10. CONQUERING DRAGONS AND KNIGHTS

YUU MIYAZAKI
ILLUSTRATION BY
okiura

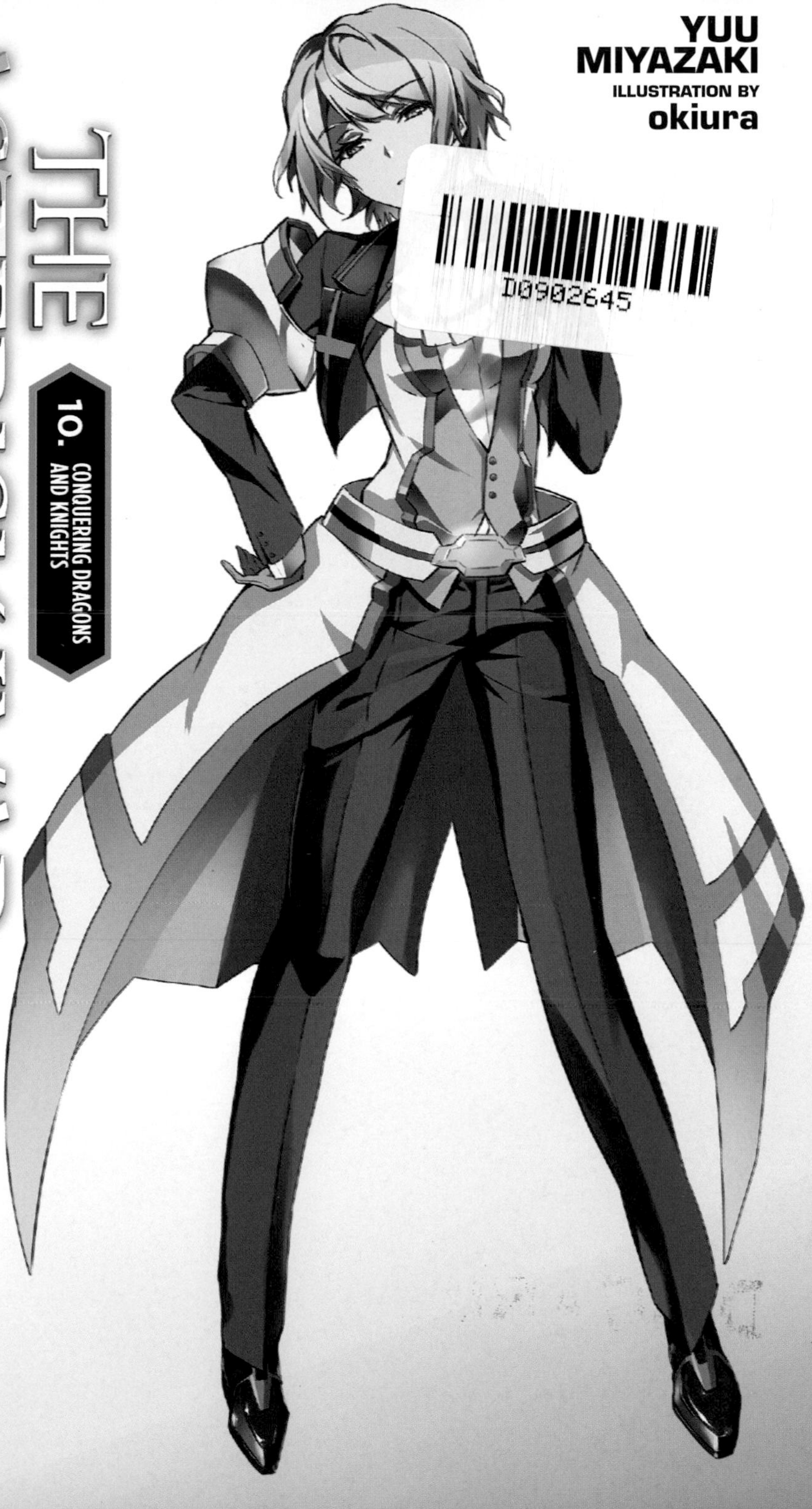

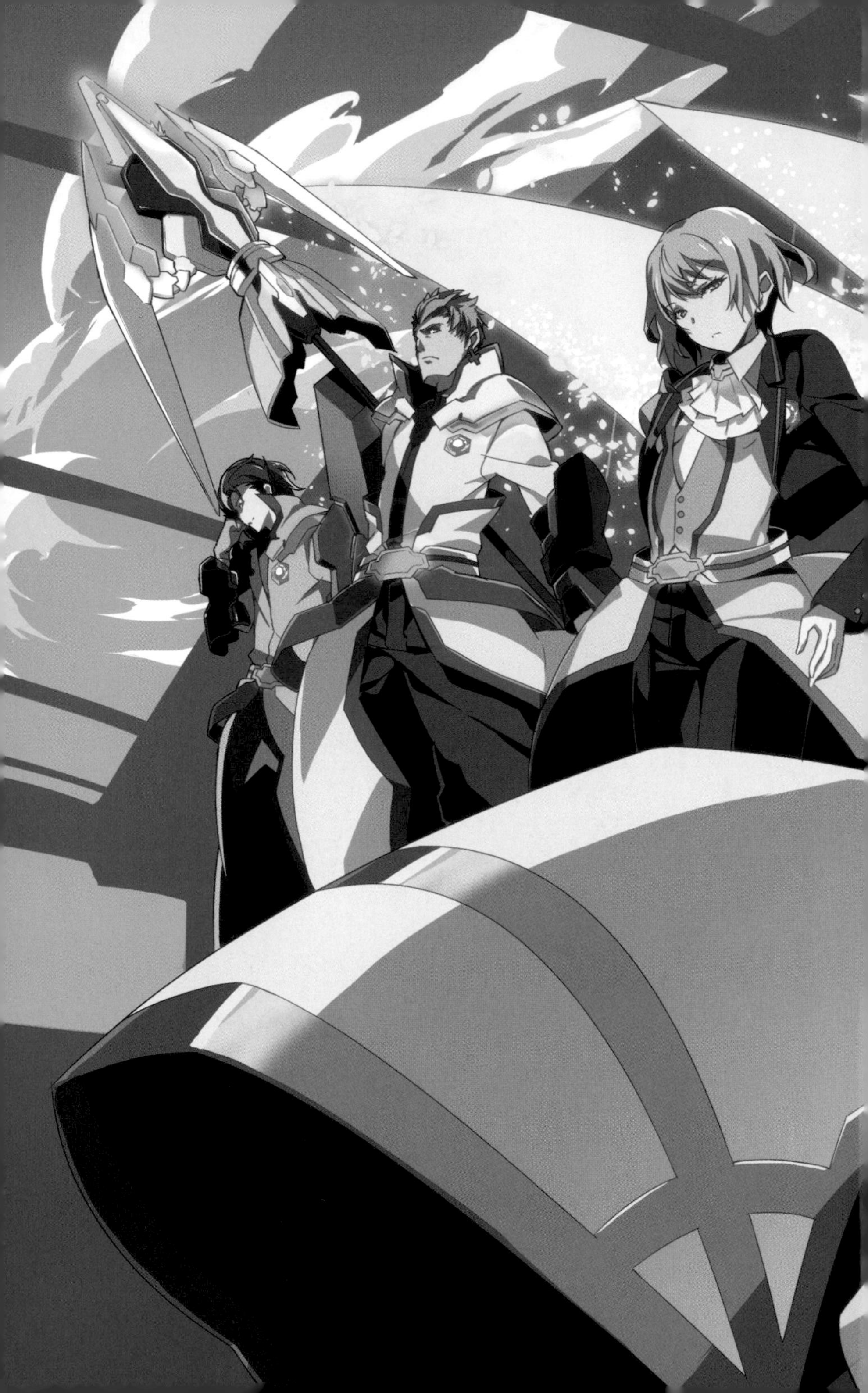

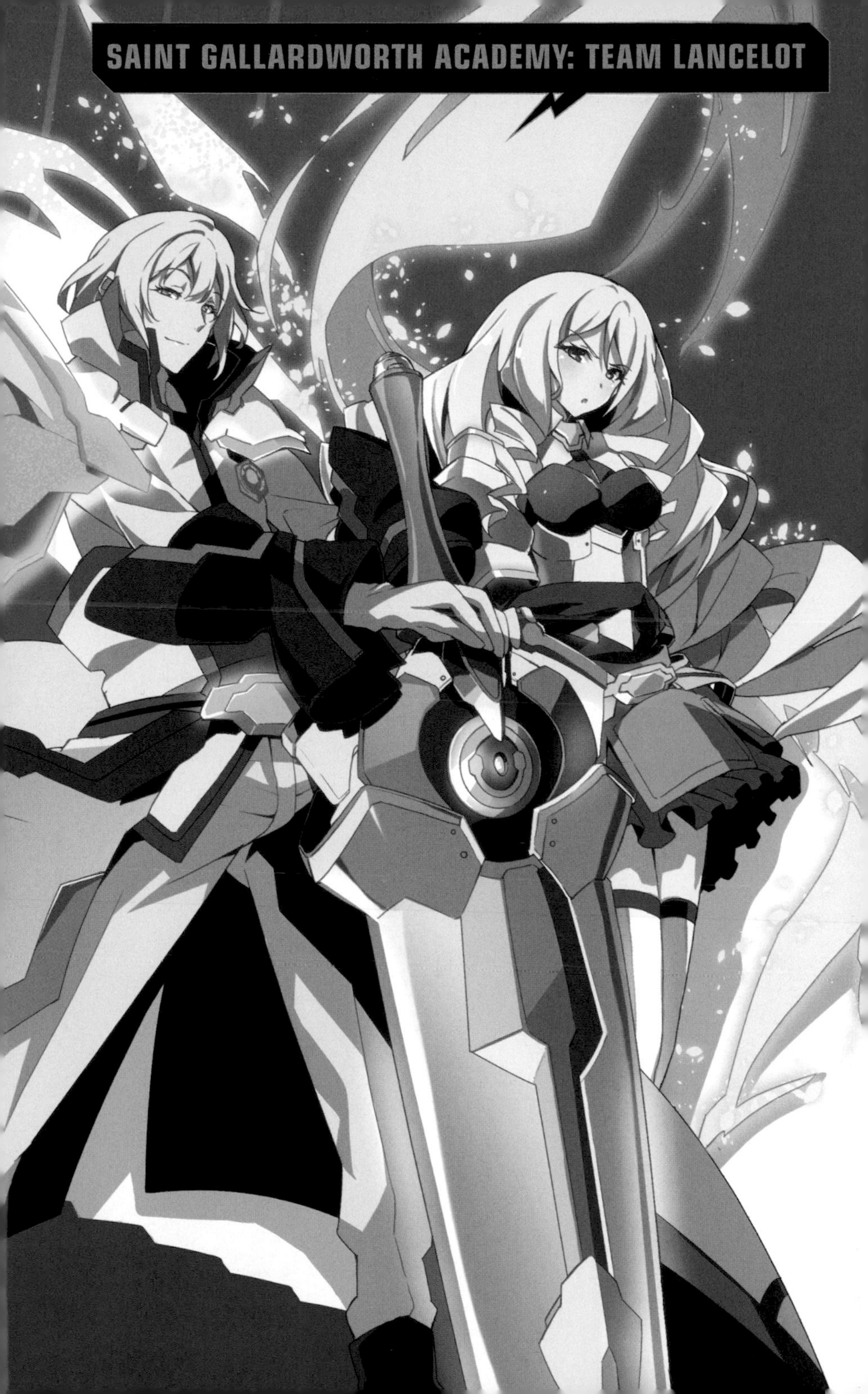
SAINT GALLARDWORTH ACADEMY: TEAM LANCELOT

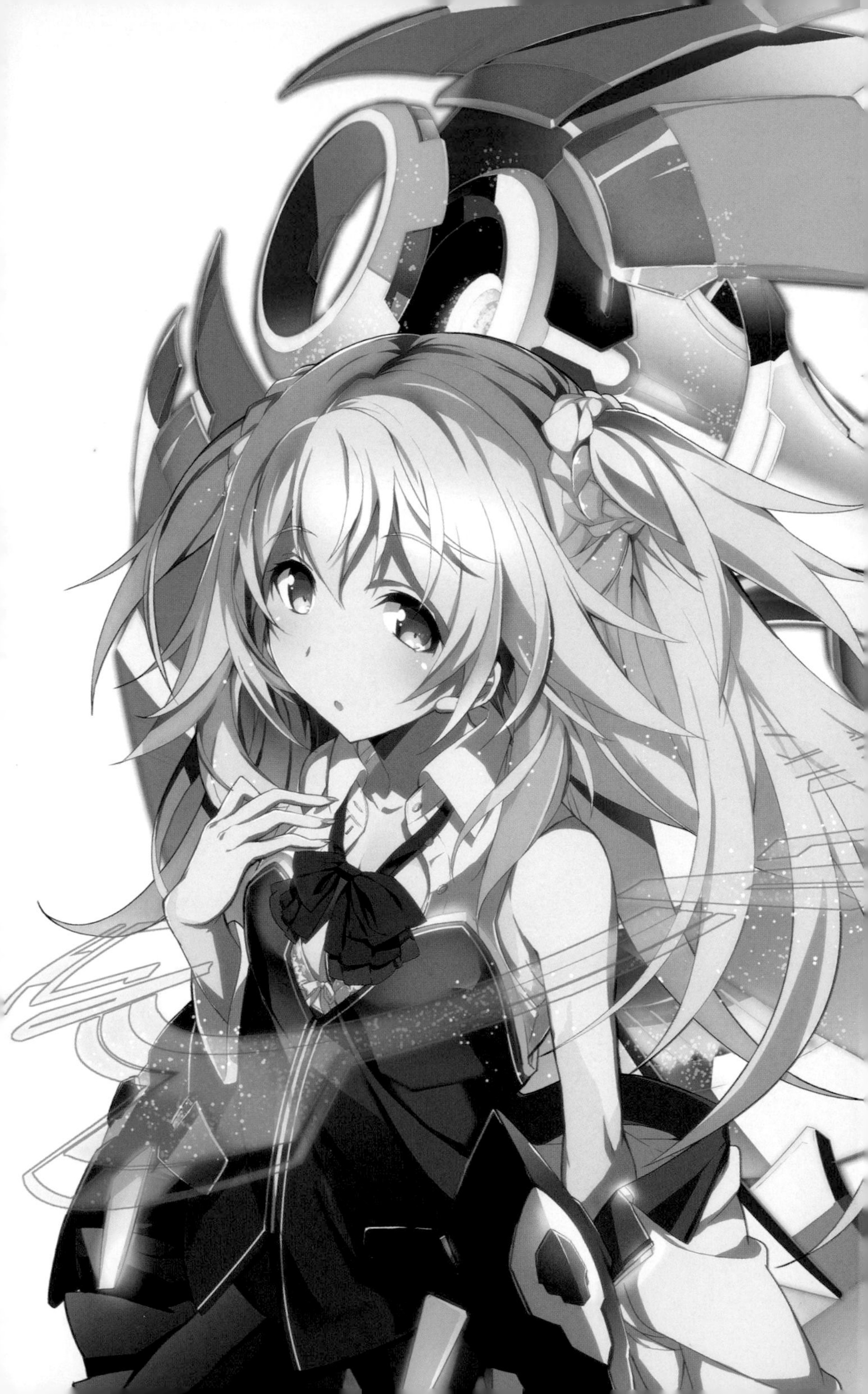

THE ASTERISK WAR

10. CONQUERING DRAGONS AND KNIGHTS

YUU MIYAZAKI
ILLUSTRATION: OKIURA

YEN ON

NEW YORK

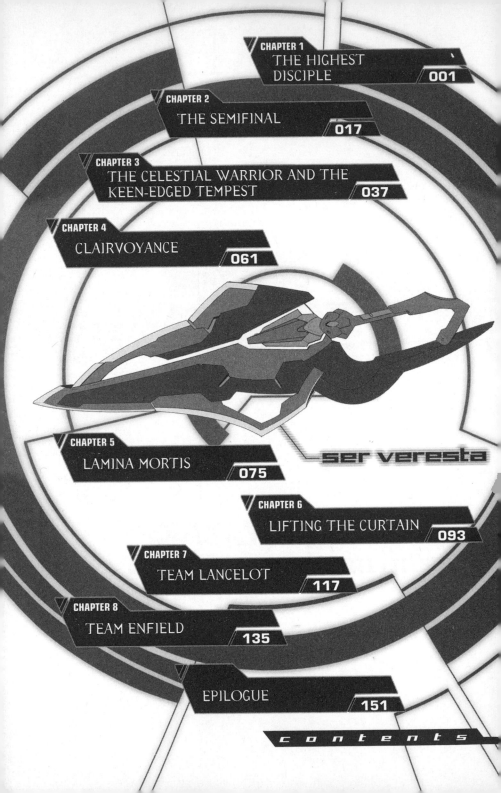

ser veresta

contents

SEIDOUKAN ACADEMY

AYATO AMAGIRI

The protagonist of this work. Wielder of the Ser Veresta. Alias Murakumo.

ALIAS: Gathering Clouds, Murakumo
ORGA LUX: Ser Veresta

JULIS-ALEXIA VON RIESSFELD

Princess of Lieseltania. Ayato's partner for the Phoenix.

ALIAS: the Witch of the Resplendent Flames, Gluhen Rose
LUX: Aspera Spina

CLAUDIA ENFIELD

Student council president at Seidoukan Academy. Leader of Team Enfield.

ALIAS: the Commander of a Thousand Visions, Parca Morta
ORGA LUX: Pan-Dora

SAYA SASAMIYA

Ayato's childhood friend. An expert in weaponry and machines.

ALIAS: none yet given
LUX: type 38 Lux grenade launcher Helnekraum, type 34 wave cannon Ark Van Ders Improved Model, and others

KIRIN TOUDOU

Disciple of the Toudou School of swordsmanship with natural talent. Saya's partner for the Phoenix.

ALIAS: the Keen-Edged Tempest, Shippuu Jinrai
LUX: none (wields the katana Senbakiri)

EISHIROU YABUKI

Ayato's roommate. Member of the newspaper club.

LESTER MACPHAIL

Number nine at Seidoukan Academy. Brusque and straightforward but has a deep sense of duty.

RANDY HOOKE

Lester's partner for the Phoenix.

KYOUKO YATSUZAKI

Ayato and company's homeroom teacher.

PREVIOUSLY IN *THE ASTERISK WAR*...

While Team Enfield prepared to face their most formidable opponents yet in the semifinals of the Gryps, the integrated enterprise foundation Galaxy targeted Claudia for assassination. Eishirou Yabuki's father, Bujinsai, pursued her in a life-or-death game of cat and mouse, and Ayato finally succeeded in removing the third lock of his seal (though for only a brief moment), thereby fending off the assailants. Claudia had dedicated her whole life to making that day's events a reality, but with the crisis averted, she decided to return to typical school life in Asterisk.

characters

THE ASTERISK WAR, Vol. 10
YUU MIYAZAKI

Translation by Haydn Trowell
Cover art by okiura

© Yuu Miyazaki 2016
First published in Japan in 2016 by KADOKAWA CORPORATION.
English translation rights reserved by Yen Press, LLC under the license from KADOKAWA CORPORATION, Tokyo, through TUTTLE-MORI AGENCY, INC. Tokyo.

English translation © 2019 by Yen Press, LLC

Yen On
1290 Avenue of the Americas
New York, NY 10104

Visit us at yenpress.com
facebook.com/yenpress
twitter.com/yenpress
yenpress.tumblr.com
instagram.com/yenpress

First Yen On Edition: June 2019

Yen On is an imprint of Yen Press, LLC.
The Yen On name and logo are trademarks of Yen Press, LLC.

The publisher is not responsible for websites (or their content) that are not owned by the publisher.

Library of Congress Cataloging-in-Publication Data
Names: Miyazaki, Yuu, author. | Tanaka, Melissa, translator. |
Trowell, Haydn, translator.
Title: The asterisk war / Yuu Miyazaki ; translation by Melissa Tanaka.
Other titles: Gakusen toshi asterisk. English
Description: First Yen On edition. | New York, NY : Yen On, 2016– |
v. 6–8 translation by Haydn Trowell | Audience: Ages 13 & up.
Identifiers: LCCN 2016023755 | ISBN 9780316315272 (v. 1 : paperback) |
ISBN 9780316398589 (v. 2 : paperback) | ISBN 9780316398602 (v. 3 : paperback) |
ISBN 9780316398626 (v. 4 : paperback) | ISBN 9780316398657 (v. 5 : paperback) |
ISBN 9780316398671 (v. 6 : paperback) | ISBN 9780316398695 (v. 7 : paperback) |
ISBN 9780316398718 (v. 8 : paperback) | ISBN 9781975302801 (v. 9 : paperback) |
ISBN 9781975329358 (v. 10 : paperback)
Subjects: CYAC: Science fiction. | BISAC: FICTION / Science Fiction / Adventure.
Classification: LCC PZ7.1.M635 As 2016 | DDC [Fic]—dc23
LC record available at https://lccn.loc.gov/2016023755

ISBNs: 978-1-9753-2935-8 (paperback)
978-1-9753-0429-4 (ebook)

1 3 5 7 9 10 8 6 4 2

LSC-C

Printed in the United States of America

CHAPTER 1
THE HIGHEST DISCIPLE

The Room of the Black Tortoise in Jie Long Seventh Institute's Hall of the Yellow Dragon:

A vast, dimly lit space filled with row upon row of stone pillars—it was among the Ban'yuu Tenra's—that is, Xinglou Fan's—favorite training areas. The ceiling towered high into the distance, the earthen floor compacted firmly by the feet of its users. The room was lit only by the gentle lights installed on each of the stone pillars, making it impossible to see just how deep the space actually was.

In the middle of that hall, two figures were squaring off.

The first was Xinglou Fan, the master of the Hall of the Yellow Dragon; the other was her highest disciple, Xiaohui Wu.

"*Pò!*"

"Hmm…!"

Xiaohui stepped forward, lunging out with a powerful strike, strong enough that, had it made contact, it ought to have thrown the body of his small opponent flying across the room. Xinglou, however, effortlessly dodged the blow.

Even so, Xiaohui didn't waste so much as a moment before spinning around, lashing out again with a wide kick.

Xinglou leaped over the strike, but at that moment, just as Xiaohui put his fingers together in a *kuji-kiri* gesture, countless needlelike barbs erupted out of the ground around her, tearing into her body still suspended in midair—or so it had seemed. In the blink of an eye, however, she had completely vanished, as if into a shimmering wall of heat.

"!"

The next moment, the figures of five separate Xinglous appeared out of nowhere around Xiaohui, lunging toward him from every direction.

Even so, his expression still betrayed no hint of emotion as he braced himself for the attack.

Her kick, however, was so powerful that it caused a small crater to explode at his feet and left the air trembling around them. And she didn't stop there; she leaped into the air once more and followed through with a series of further strikes, flowing from first one blow to the next.

"...!"

Xiaohui withstood them all, not yielding an inch, before countering with a kick of his own that managed to throw Xinglou higher into the air—

But no. Xinglou, it seemed, had by her own accord leaped yet higher in reaction to the strike.

She muttered something as she glided down, and a barrage of burning fireballs materialized around her, crashing toward him.

Xiaohui dodged them all—so easily, it seemed, that his movements should have been impossible for a person of his large frame—before using one of the stone pillars as a launching pad to throw himself into the air as he lunged at his opponent.

Xinglou moved to meet his attack head-on.

"...No matter how many times I watch them, I still can't really believe it..."

"It's beyond words..."

Shenyun Li and Shenhua Li, watching the bout from across the hall, let out sighs of admiration.

"Tell me about it." Cecily Wong nodded in agreement. "Their martial arts are one thing, but the power of those seals and incantations—and without having to resort to using charms or anything like that, either… They're both really something, right?"

If Cecily, who led the Water sect, thought as much, there could be no doubting the two fighters' skills in *seisenjutsu*.

"But shouldn't we get them to call it off? We *do* have a match coming up later today…," Hufeng Zhao pointed out to the other members of his team.

Today was, after all, the day of the semifinals. True, they still had practically half of that day to go before it got underway, but it wouldn't do for Xiaohui to end up getting injured before it had even begun.

"HAH, YOU REALLY THINK YOU CAN GET IN THE MIDDLE OF THOSE TWO? I'D LIKE TO SEE YOU TRY." Alema Seiyng laughed silently, her words projected in a nearby air-window as she leaned against one of the room's many pillars with her arms crossed.

As far as Hufeng was concerned, Alema's attitude was as irreverent as ever, but seeing as she wasn't technically one of Xinglou's disciples, he couldn't really complain.

"…Why don't you go back to your room and get some rest?" was all he could respond with as he tried to find a diplomatic excuse to convince her to leave.

In fact, it was no exaggeration to say that her bandage-wrapped body was completely riddled with injuries. That had been the result of the job she had carried out for Xinglou just the day before, so she hadn't really had any time to rest and recover.

"HAH, ARE YOU WORRIED ABOUT ME? I GUESS I WILL—ONCE THEY'RE DONE," she quipped with a grin. Her grit was nothing short of incredible.

"By the way, Alema," Cecily began.

"Yeah? What is it?"

It was clear from the casual way in which they spoke to each other that the two were on good terms.

"How long have you been able to watch master and Elder Brother train with each other?"

"WELL, I'M FREE TO COME AND GO AS I PLEASE, RIGHT?"

The members of Hufeng's Team Yellow Dragon had only recently been granted permission to observe Xinglou and Xiaohui's training matches. Alema, on the other hand, appeared to have been able to do so for a while now. Hufeng felt more than a touch of jealousy at that fact.

"It's just that, doesn't something seem different?" Cecily continued. "She doesn't look like her normal self, you know, when she's training with Elder Brother..."

"Ah, that..." Alema frowned.

"Ah, we also thought—"

"—that something was up."

The twins turned toward Alema.

"She always looks like she's having fun when she trains with us, right? But I don't know, maybe it's different when she's with Elder Brother...?"

"Isn't it just that she can't afford to let her guard down, seeing how strong he is?" Hufeng replied.

Cecily bit her lip, as if she couldn't accept that answer. "You can't be serious, Hufeng? You've seen her—she always smiles whenever there's a new challenger wanting to become a disciple, no matter how strong they are. If strength even comes into it, isn't she the type to just get more excited the stronger her opponent is?"

"Well... I guess so."

There was no arguing the point. Xinglou would probably be the happiest person alive if she could square off against someone stronger than her—the question was more that Hufeng doubted whether such a person existed.

"Well, in that case, why...?"

"...Mm, this is just what she said, in praise, I guess. Basically, 'He's my greatest failure.' Or something like that," Alema said uncomfortably, averting her gaze as she scratched at her head.

"Her greatest failure...?"

That didn't make any sense.

Out of all her disciples, Xiaohui ought to have been her greatest masterpiece. As much as Hufeng hated to admit it, neither he nor Cecily, nor any of Xinglou's other disciples for that matter, could compare.

"Well, I might have said too much. Anyway, it looks like they're finished, so I'll be off."

When Hufeng glanced back toward the two, their bout did indeed seem to be over. The floor was gouged out in places, and several of the stone pillars lay collapsed, strewn around the room—but despite all that, neither Xiaohui, nor, of course, Xinglou, looked to have suffered any sort of injury.

Hufeng let out a sigh of relief.

"Huh?! Alema?!" Cecily called out.

Hufeng spun around at the sound of her voice, only to find that Alema had already disappeared. She must have run off just as they had all turned their attention to Xinglou. As always, he had been completely unable to sense her departure.

"Oh-ho... Here you are," Xinglou greeted them, Xiaohui following along behind her.

At that moment, they all fell to their knees in obeisance.

"Master, Elder Brother, what a wonderful performance," Hufeng, as their representative, replied.

Xinglou flashed him a knowing smile. "Nonsense, Hufeng. You were all busy talking toward the end."

"Ugh! Th-that's...!"

Hufeng had no idea how she could have realized that, but there was no use trying to deny it.

"Fret not. Truth be told, there was little to learn from today's bout."

"M-master...?" Hufeng shook his head vehemently.

Xinglou merely sighed. "It's just a worn-out routine."

"..."

He glanced toward Xiaohui, who merely stood behind their master expressionlessly. Hufeng could only wonder what he could be thinking.

"More importantly, today you will be facing those children from Seidoukan. I'm looking forward to it. Don't disappoint me."

"Of course not, master. We won't lose."

"We'll be sure to give you a match to be proud of."

The twins, their heads bowed meekly, were as cavalier as ever.

"Hmph. I'm not interested in whether you win or lose. What matters is how you perform."

"Of course, we understand that. You haven't given us any crazy orders this time, so without any restrictions on our strategies, we'll definitely be able to make it a match to remember," Cecily boasted. While maybe not to Alema's extent, she, too, wasn't the kind to shy around their master.

"Oh-ho, then I shall look forward to it. Ah, Xiaohui, come and see me before you go."

"...Very well," Xiaohui replied, his head bowed.

With a passing glance toward him, Xinglou clicked her fingers, vanishing as if she had been, from the very beginning, no more than a cloud of smoke.

*

"I'm terribly sorry for what happened. I'd like to apologize to you all once again," Claudia said, head bowed, as her team members arrived at their prep room on the day of their semifinal match.

The four other members of Team Enfield glanced toward one another at this extraordinary show of contrition.

Ayato had been expecting Julis to come out with two or three more minor complaints in addition to those that she had delivered the previous night, but at this sight, all she could do was let out a nervous cough and put her hands to her hips. "W-well, it's over and done with. Anyway, are you up to it?"

"I think so. The healers at the hospital really are amazing. And we haven't faced any penalties, either," Claudia replied with a light laugh.

Treatment from healers certainly was effective, but teams that relied on it during the Festa normally incurred some manner of penalty for doing so. In particular, if the injuries had been incurred during a Festa match, participants who received such healing could be disqualified from further competition.

Nonetheless, for someone to even receive such treatment, their life had to be in danger anyway, so in such cases, there really was no other choice.

"That said, I can't say that everything is perfect..."

The wound in Claudia's chest was completely healed, but her other injuries, not to mention her fatigue, still remained. It would be an exaggeration to say that she was in prime fighting condition.

"But still, I'm more worried about all of you. None of you overdid it yesterday, did you?"

To be fair, while she might not have been at her best, he could say the same thing about himself and the others.

Ayato had squared off in a bitter contest against Eishirou's father, Bujinsai, while Julis, Saya, and Kirin had fought against both Shadowstar and the seemingly close-to-immortal members of the Yabuki clan. None had received any serious injuries, but the ordeal had left them all exhausted.

Julis and Ayato were in particularly bad shape. Julis had gone all out with her abilities, while Ayato had been forced to break his seal. It wasn't as bad as the first time he had done so—he could still move around, even if his body felt heavier than usual—but he didn't know how well he would be able to fight in the upcoming match.

"Well, we'll just have to do what we can," he said.

Saya, standing beside him, nodded. "Right. What matters now is working out how to win today. So, Claudia... We need a strategy."

"Unfortunately," Julis cut in with a downcast note to her voice, "we're probably going to have a hard time standing up to Team Yellow Dragon like this."

"I understand. In that case..."

"Ah! Um, before that..." Kirin, who until that moment had been waiting in silence, timidly raised her hand. "C-Claudia, is the… Is the Pan-Dora…?"

At that question, they all turned toward her. Yesterday's attack by the Night Emit—indeed, even the dream she had so catastrophically sought to make reality—could be traced back to that Orga Lux, the Pan-Dora. All five knew that.

It wouldn't be at all surprising if she was to want nothing more to do with it—in fact, that would be the most natural course of action.

But Claudia merely shone with a composed smile as she unsheathed the Orga Lux's activators from their holders at her waist. "Yes. I don't blame this darling at all. And if we want to win, we're going to need its abilities."

"If that's what you think, I won't try to argue with you, but still…" Julis looked as if she wasn't particularly convinced.

To be honest, Ayato thought the same way. No matter how extraordinary its abilities, the Pan-Dora was simply too dangerous.

"Ah-ha, there's no need to worry," Claudia said with a soft laugh. "Given what's happened, I won't blame you if you don't believe me, but for now at least, I want to try to understand how to get along better with it. I still don't believe that I've been quite capable of drawing out all its power."

"…What do you mean?" Saya asked. "You think the Pan-Dora has another ability?"

Claudia shook her head. "It's just a feeling, that's all."

"Come on. Stop playing around," Julis interjected.

"Anyway, there's no need to worry about me. Even if something was to happen, I have all of you here to help me."

Claudia may have tried to pass that off as a joke, but Ayato knew she was trying to hide her embarrassment. She had changed, it seemed.

"However, and I'm terribly sorry about this, but I only have around sixty seconds left in my precognition stock. I ended up using quite a lot of it to evade the Night Emit… So I only plan to use it to avoid attacks. That goes for our next match, too, of course."

The Pan-Dora was, by nature, better suited for defense than

offense, as while it allowed its user to test possible outcomes through trial and error, the more complicated the course of events, the greater the number of opportunities that became available.

"So what's our strategy for the semifinal?" Julis continued.

"Now, now, there's no need to rush," Claudia replied calmly before taking a swig of the drink she had brought with her. "Fortunately, we still have some time to spare, so why don't we all take a breather first?"

It was currently around noon.

Their match had originally been scheduled for early evening, but seeing as the other semifinal match, which had been due to begin afterward, had been canceled, theirs had been moved back to compensate. That gave them more time to rest and ample opportunity to work out how to proceed.

"Hmm… I guess I *might* be rushing into things a bit too quickly." Julis sighed.

"A-ah… Yes, let's try to calm down first," Kirin added, letting herself relax.

There had been so much going on over the past day that they all still seemed somewhat on edge.

"In that case, there's something else I want to get out of the way," Saya began, raising her hand. "Claudia confessed to Ayato, right? I want to know what happened next."

"Bffft?!" Ayato blurted.

"What?!" Claudia exclaimed, almost spilling her drink. Her face turned red, and she had lifted both hands to her cheeks to cover them as she gasped for breath—before slowly turning toward Saya with a tremble. "Wh-what on earth are you saying?"

Ayato had never seen her act this way before, and Julis and Kirin must have been just as surprised as he was, because they both stared at her suspiciously.

"Well, if you think about what happened, if you think about *why* it happened, even Ayato ought to have realized it by now."

"Th-that's true…," Claudia murmured as she averted her gaze.

There was something indescribably cute about the reaction.

"Um, Saya... The thing is...," Ayato began, trying to explain, when Claudia held out a hand to stop him.

"Ah..." She took a deep breath to calm her nerves and put a hand to her chest, though her cheeks were still tinged red. "As far as I'm concerned, my thoughts were rather disorganized, and I wasn't able to convey my feelings the way I would have liked," she declared clearly. "Which is why, one day, I intend to properly tell Ayato how I feel. That's all!"

Saya gave a slow nod. "I see. That's good enough for me... In other words, I still have the advantage. That's a relief."

"I don't know what to say... You really are impressive." Claudia stared back at her in grudging admiration.

"Feel free to praise me more often."

"No, I wouldn't say that I was praising you, exactly... But oh well, I guess we can call it that."

"Come on, this isn't the time to be worrying about that kind of thing!" Julis suddenly cried out, as if she couldn't bear to listen to the two anymore.

Julis's flustered expression was so endearing it rivaled Claudia's from a moment ago.

The same went for Kirin, standing beside her.

"Th-that's right...!" she stammered. "Claudia, what about the match...?"

"Ah, yes. In that case..." She pulled out her mobile and cleared her voice. "Let's start with a simple analysis. To start with, all five members of Team Yellow Dragon are highly capable close-combat martial artists. However, because of that, they don't place significant emphasis on teamwork. It seems they prioritize individual decision-making over group coordination." With that, she opened five air-windows displaying the profiles of their opponents. "This isn't to say that there's no division of roles between them. The Li twins, whom Ayato and Julis fought during the Phoenix, effectively serve to support the other team members. It's safe to say that their illusionary *seisenjutsu* techniques are extremely effective in team situations."

"Do you mean they're supporting the others, even without coordinating?" Kirin wondered aloud.

Claudia nodded. "Their techniques create opportunities that their team members can then use to their advantage. That said, it can't really be called coordination."

"I see…"

"That being the case, I'll be the one to take care of those two," Claudia declared.

"Huh?" Ayato startled. "By yourself?"

Certainly, the twins might not be as powerful as the others, but they were still formidable opponents. Ayato knew that from experience. Moreover, they excelled at controlling the conditions of the arena. They would be even more dangerous if they could afford to leave offense to someone else.

"Of course, I'll need Julis and Saya to support me whenever possible, but I'm the one best suited to take them both on."

"Best suited? What does that mean?"

"It's simple, really," Claudia replied indifferently. "My personality is even worse than theirs."

Ayato didn't know whether to nod along to that or not, but there was no denying that none of the others would be capable of seeing through their tricks the way she could. In that respect, at least, he and Julis had been completely bested during their encounter with them in the Phoenix.

"However, Julis and Saya will also be facing Raigeki Senka and Tenka Musou as well, so you'll both need to consider them as your highest priority," Claudia added as she enlarged two of the air-windows.

The first held a picture of Cecily Wong, a young woman with European features—a rarity at Jie Long—while the second was Hufeng Zhao, whom Ayato had met during the Gran Colosseo.

The air-windows soon changed to recordings of a match. They had already watched it several times before, and so, Ayato immediately recognized it as the pair's championship match at the Phoenix four years earlier.

At that time, Cecily had yet to learn *seisenjutsu*, so the pair had fought with the kind of martial arts typical of students from Jie Long.

In broad terms, Cecily excelled in power and Hufeng in speed.

Even back then, Hufeng had moved incredibly quickly.

"They've no doubt become much stronger since this recording."

"Hmm... We've no shortage of opponents, so why choose Saya and me?" Julis asked.

"Are we well suited to facing them or something?" Saya added.

"No, I'm afraid not. It merely comes down to the process of elimination."

Julis blinked in surprise at this admission, quickly breaking out into a deep frown. "What does that mean? You'd better not be playing around."

"There's no hidden meaning behind it. We need you to hold those two down at all costs. Because you see..." Claudia paused there, turning to face their two still unaccounted-for members. "We need Ayato and Kirin to take care of the last one, Hagun Seikun... Although, I'm not sure whether even the both of you together will be able to beat him."

At this, the four all caught their breath.

"...Right, Xiaohui Wu...," Julis whispered.

It went without saying that Xiaohui Wu was strong. Overwhelmingly strong.

Ayato and Kirin were among the highest-ranked close-combat fighters in all of Asterisk, but there was every chance that even they, fighting together, might not be enough to defeat him.

"B-but Ayato has the Ser Veresta," Kirin pointed out as she stepped forward.

"Right, that should count to our advantage," Ayato added. "Xiaohui Wu and the other *daoshi* are basically just Dantes. They shouldn't have any Orga Luxes of their own."

Stregas and Dantes were said to be ill-suited to using Orga Luxes.

"And you said that Ayato undid his third seal yesterday. In that case—"

"Ah, no, I mean… Doing that again will be…difficult."

Saya was talking about when he had repulsed Eishirou's father, Bujinsai. Ayato had already explained it all to everyone, and he doubted he would be able to pull it off again.

His sister, Haruka, seemed to have placed her seal on him in stages. Ayato had yet to satisfy the conditions necessary to release the last one fully—though he had a vague feeling that he was coming close.

That being the case, he wanted to avoid breaking through the seal by force, as he had the previous night.

He had probably only been able to do so then because he had been so desperate to save Claudia. The simple truth was that he didn't think he would be able to open that door again under normal circumstances.

"Ayato's strength was indeed incredible when he did that… But it's an uncertain factor. We can't rely on it in our strategy."

"There's no getting around that," Julis muttered in agreement.

"Anyway, Hagun Seikun will be their team leader, just like during their previous matches. In other words, we can't win unless we can defeat him. So we're all counting on you both."

"Got it. We'll figure something out," Ayato declared.

"R-right! I—I'll… We'll do our best!" Kirin nodded in agreement.

"Of course, this is just an outline of sorts, so make sure that you're all aware of what the others are doing at all times and support them as necessary. As far as more specific coordination patterns are concerned…"

And with that, the five spent the entire remainder of their time before the match preparing their strategy.

*

"Mmm, delicious! There truly is no beating your tea!"

They were within Xinglou's private quarters, in a room situated in an elegant tower surrounded by a wide garden overflowing with flowers.

Of all her disciples, only Xiaohui had been granted permission to enter this place—although that being said, no one else would even have been able to find it. The spaces within the Hall of the Yellow Dragon expanded and twisted in seemingly impossible ways, with this section in its deepest, innermost recesses being the most confounding of all.

Outside, with autumn approaching, the air was becoming cooler with each passing day, but in here, it was a perpetual spring.

And amid that suspended landscape was something that never failed to rekindle Xiaohui's distant memories and make his heart ache.

"Xiaohui, would you pour me another?" asked Xinglou, sitting atop a chair beside a window, her childlike legs swinging back and forth.

"…As you wish."

Xiaohui, who until that moment had been waiting patiently behind her, gathered the tea utensils and began to prepare another cup.

After giving it some consideration, he decided to brew a pot of Huangshan Maofeng tea. Xinglou's tastes could be unpredictable; there were times when she would tell him directly what she wanted, and others when she would leave everything to him. Comparatively speaking, the latter tended to be more common. As if she expected him to see right through her and read her desires.

Right, Xinglou only tended to put the bare necessities into words.

That was why he was always at a loss as to what to do.

What could he do to satisfy her?

He was, after all, just a foolish, ignorant disciple, unable to answer that ever-pressing question.

All he could do was pick out the tea that he thought would best suit her tastes at any given moment.

"Sorry to keep you waiting, master."

"Oh-ho… What a splendid aroma." Xinglou brought the cup to her lips, her eyes narrowing in contentment.

There was no bitterness in that yellow-green tea. It was mellow in flavor, with a faint sweetness that he had suspected would please her current mood.

"Now then… Xiaohui," began Xinglou, turning her eyes toward him.

"…Master?

"I'm looking forward to your semifinal match," she said tenderly.

However, there was something behind her words that sent his brain turning.

Of course, he would do the same thing he always did. No matter the situation, he always put everything he had into serving her.

But he understood there was a deeper meaning behind her words.

"I will put my very soul into it."

"…Hmm." Xinglou nodded in apparent satisfaction before casually putting her fingers together in a symbolic gesture.

At that moment, a streak of light ran through the center of the room, and as if it had been there all along, a space opened up before him.

It was his prep room in the Sirius Dome.

The other members of Team Yellow Dragon were all kneeling inside. Xiaohui turned to his master, placing his right fist in his left palm as a gesture of obeisance, before stepping forth to join them.

CHAPTER 2
THE SEMIFINAL

"A-ah, I'm so sorry! I—I need to go the bathroom...!" Kirin, who had been acting restless for a while now, gave them all a polite bow and sped out of the prep room.

They had just finished their strategy meeting and were about to enter the arena.

"..."

After a short moment, Ayato stood up, too, quickly facing his remaining team members. "Uh, sorry. I'll be back in a minute."

It didn't take Claudia long to understand what he meant. "Thank you, Ayato." She nodded.

He stepped outside, scanning his surroundings. Seeing as this section of the Sirius Dome was off-limits to everyone except contestants, even his highly tuned senses could not detect anyone nearby.

There was only the dull, roaring excitement of the many tens of thousands of spectators who had come to watch the match, like a deep rumbling somewhere off in the distance.

Turning down the corridor in the opposite direction of the stage, it didn't take him long to find Kirin.

She was leaning against the wall with her eyes closed, as if to mentally prepare herself for the upcoming battle.

"Kirin...," Ayato called out softly.

"—! A-Ayato…!" She opened her eyes with a start, clearly taken by surprise.

Ayato flashed her an apologetic smile. "Are you worried about the match?"

"That isn't it," she replied, her hands gripping the hilt of the Senbakiri tightly. "I'm just nervous for some reason."

Kirin certainly had a reserved and shy personality, but she also wasn't the kind of person to lose her nerve over an upcoming match.

No matter how strong the opponents she faced were, she wasn't inclined to regret her actions, even if they resulted in defeat—that was the kind of swordswoman she was.

"Um… I've just been thinking about some things."

"Some things…?"

"I mean… I'm not just fighting for myself in this match."

So that's it.

There was no mistaking that being part of a team required entering a different state of mind than fighting alone.

All the more so when you were the one responsible for facing Hagun Seikun, Jie Long's renowned Celestial Warrior.

Kirin's reason for participating in the Gryps was to help her father, but both he and Julis had their own reasons, too.

Julis was fighting for her country.

Ayato was fighting for his sister.

While the situation was different for Claudia and Saya, they, too, had their own reasons for taking part.

With so many weights on each of their shoulders, it was only natural to feel troubled.

"…You really are kindhearted, Kirin," Ayato said softly as he placed a hand on her head.

"Ah…" She looked up at him in surprise before quickly glancing down at her feet with a faint smile. "It feels like it's been a long time since you patted me on the head."

"…Has it, now?"

That hadn't occurred to him, but when he thought about it, she did seem to be right.

They remained that way for a long moment, until Kirin glanced up toward him, meeting his eyes. "Thanks for thinking about me, Ayato. But I'll be okay. To tell you the truth, I'm not just nervous."

"Huh?"

"It makes me happy, too, that I can help carry the team on my shoulders," she said clearly, looking straight at him.

There was no hint of hesitation or doubt in her voice.

"Ha-ha, maybe I was worrying too much."

Kirin was strong.

Stronger than he had realized. Much stronger.

"N-n-not at all…! I mean, you've helped cheer me up!" she replied, waving her hands and bowing her head.

"I see… In that case, we should probably head back. The others are waiting for us."

"Right…"

Ayato led the way, with Kirin trailing along behind him.

"…"

"Huh?" He looked over his shoulder, thinking that she had murmured something.

"Ah, no, it's nothing…!"

He had heard something, though. He was sure of it…

"Hurry up, you two!" came Julis's voice echoing down the corridor. She, Claudia, and Saya were all waiting outside the prep room.

"We should hurry. It's about to start," Claudia said.

"We'll be disqualified if we're late," Saya added.

"That doesn't sound very convincing, coming from you, though…," Julis remarked.

They spoke in their usual, easygoing manner.

Kirin, watching on, broke out into a laugh.

"You don't look nervous at all," Ayato noted.

"Not anymore," she replied with a smile.

Ayato let out a relieved sigh before turning to the others. "All right, then. Let's win this."

*

"*And here we are, the one and only semifinal of the twenty-fourth Gryps!*" Mico Yanase's voice echoed throughout the Sirius Dome. "*We only have two matches to go until we find out who will be this year's champions! The winners of this match will face off against Team Lancelot, who have advanced to the championship by default. Which of our two teams today will come out on top? At the east gate, we have the team that includes the tag partners that conquered last year's Phoenix, who you'll all remember from their last extraordinary match against Queenvale's Team Rusalka! It's Seidoukan Academy's first team to make it to the best four in the Gryps in years, Team Enfield!*"

The galleries were, as expected, full to bursting. As soon as the gate swung open, Ayato and company were all but engulfed by the thunderous cheers of the crowds.

As they all stepped out onto the bridge that led to the stage, Ayato reflexively lifted his hand to shade himself from the glaring spotlights.

"*The team leader looks to be contestant Enfield. Rumor has it that she had to be hospitalized due to some kind of trouble yesterday, but she must be feeling well enough if she can venture out here today.*"

Shizuna Hiiragi, one of the tournament's commentators this year, seemed to be well-informed. If it had reached her, then the information was probably making the rounds at the other schools, too.

"*And now, from the west gate, we have a team composed entirely of Page Ones! Organized around Xiaohui Wu, who in the preliminaries defeated Seidoukan's Team Chionothýella single-handed, and with all five members specializing in attack, they make for one of the most aggressive teams we've seen yet! It's Jie Long Seventh Institute's Team Yellow Dragon!*"

"*Contestant Wu is their team leader again this time. Thanks to his spectacular defeat of Seidoukan's Team Chionothýella, including that school's fourth-ranked fighter, Hrimthurs, he's been the center of everyone's expectations for this match. But we should also keep an eye on contestant Wong, whose fighting skills as a daoshi are nothing short of incredible. And of course, we also have contestant Zhao, with his overwhelming speed and martial arts prowess.*"

"*Those two were the winners of the Phoenix before last! After their unexpected victory over everyone's favorite tag team from Le Wolfe, they continued all the way to claim the championship!*"

"*I wonder how much further they've developed over the past four years? I suppose we'll find out today.*"

As Team Yellow Dragon entered the stage, Shizuna's commentary was all but drowned out by the tremendous roar that rose up from the galleries.

"...What's that?" Julis asked with suspicion as they watched their opponents enter the stage.

Ayato, of course, didn't know the answer.

"What is it, Ms. Hiiragi?"

"There's something strange about contestant Zhao's feet... Is that...?"

Ayato and the others had already entered the stage and were waiting for Team Yellow Dragon to join them. Claudia was the first to understand what was going on.

"It can't be..."

"*The Tongtianzu!*" Hiiragi exclaimed.

At that moment, a lone figure leaped over the bridge leading onto the stage, pirouetting through the air.

As the bridges leading onto the stage extended out of the gates at either side of the arena, they were much higher up than the stage itself. While they weren't so high that a Genestella wouldn't be able to make the jump, that figure—Hufeng Zhao—spun nimbly over it, seemingly rebounding off a series of orange bursts of light that materialized in the air.

"—!"

Of course, there was nothing there for him to leap off from.

Hufeng landed softly in the middle of the stage before turning his gaze toward Ayato and the others.

"Who would have thought you liked making an entrance so much, Tenka Musou," Julis called out.

"This kind of flashy performance isn't really my thing, but it would have been cowardly of me not to show you all this in advance,"

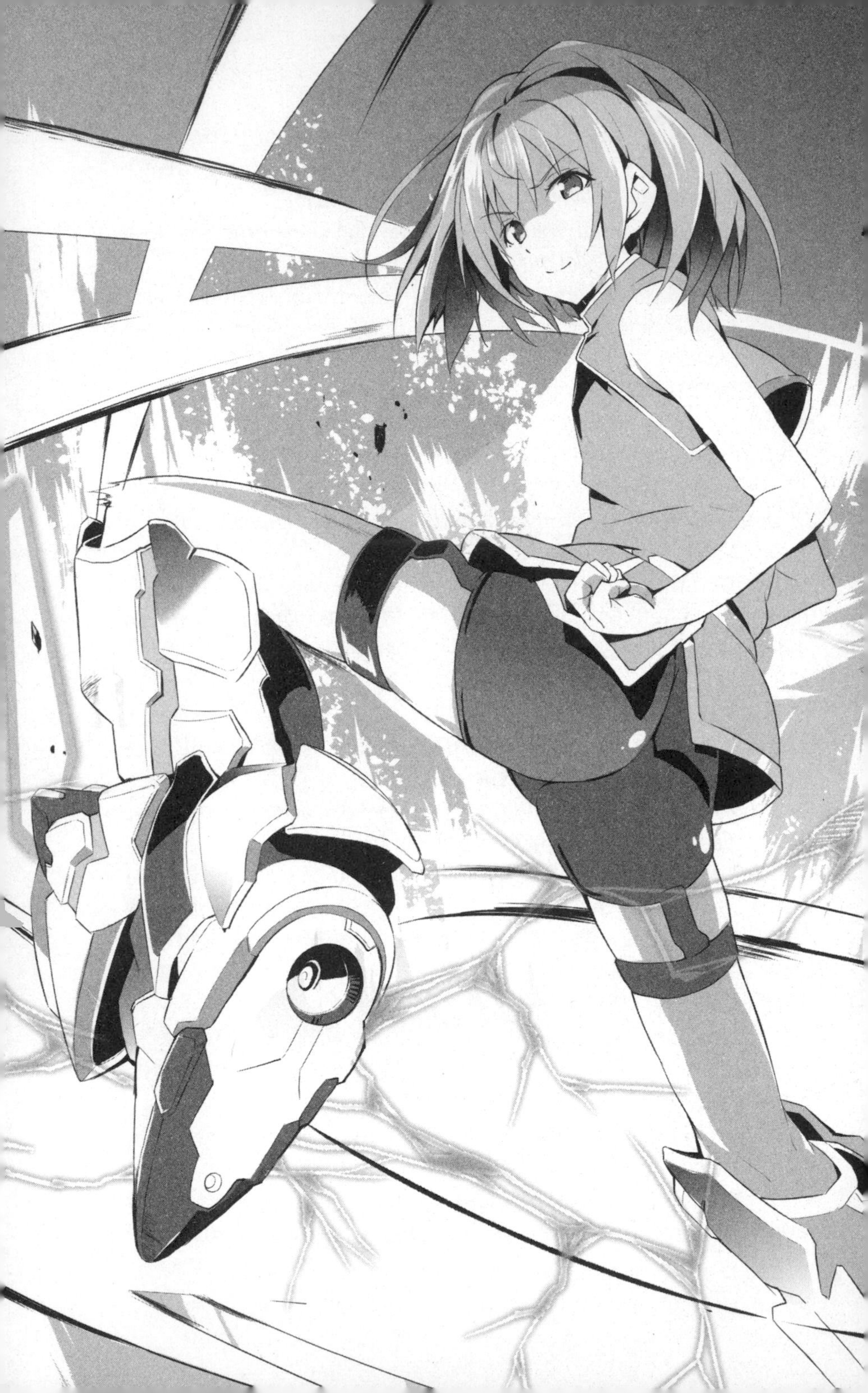

Hufeng responded, lifting one of the oddly shaped steel shoes that entirely covered his feet and went up to his shins. A deep-orange light emanated from the top of his insteps.

"Claudia," Ayato whispered. "That's urm-manadite, isn't it? Which means…?"

"Yes, it's an Orga Lux. This might be a problem… I wasn't expecting anything like this." There was an unusual tone to her voice, something bordering on self-reproach.

"Ah, the Tongtianzu is one of Jie Long's most powerful Orga Luxes, isn't it?"

"Yes. It used to be called Hermes's Talaria back when it belonged to Le Wolfe, but Jie Long has supposedly made some improvements. It's said to grant its wearer the ability to literally run through the sky."

"An Orga Lux that lets you run through the sky…?" Kirin whispered, her expression grave.

"Yes… If all you look at are its abilities, the Tongtianzu isn't a particularly powerful Orga Lux," Claudia began with a forced smile. "If all it did was effectively give its user the ability to fly, anyone with abilities like Julis would still be able to defeat them, as I'm sure Le Wolfe knew all too well. However… If you give them to an already powerful martial artist, they would turn into an incredibly powerful advantage. On that point, the people we would least want to get their hands on them have managed to do so."

"We don't have many Orga Luxes at Jie Long, and we haven't tended to give them the respect that they deserve," Hufeng called out to them, biting his lip in apparent frustration. "*Daoshi* aren't suited to using them, and martial artists don't like to rely on weapons, you see. So feel free to think of them as evidence of my own weaknesses."

"…Mastery of one's tools is its own kind of strength. It isn't something to be ashamed of," Saya said, glaring back at him.

Hufeng blinked in surprise, his expression softening as he turned her way. "Thank you, Miss Sasamiya. I was talking only about myself, of course… About my own shallow fixation on victory. I meant no offense."

"Hmm, you've got a sense of sportsmanship, at least," Julis declared, her lips puckering in a grin. "But *we* aren't going to go easy on *you*, either."

Song and Luo, whom she and Ayato had fought during the Phoenix, had been like that, too. It was the kind of personality that one could bring oneself to appreciate in one's opponents.

"The same goes for you, Glühen Rose."

"We're looking forward to paying you back for the Phoenix."

"Hmm…?"

The twins called out to them in challenge as the Jie Long team finally made its way onto the stage.

Unlike when she had addressed Hufeng, Julis's expression now was one of clear displeasure. "If that's what you want," she called back, arms crossed. "I've got a score to settle with you, too."

"Technically, it was Ayato Amagiri who beat us."

"We don't have anything to settle with *you*."

The twins leered up at her, their shoulders shaking with laughter.

"We're counting on you, Julis," Claudia murmured sharply. "Don't let them get the better of you."

Julis took a step back, her face turning slightly red. "I know that. This isn't enough to provoke me."

"Good… Make sure you watch out for their tricks."

"Don't speak too soon, Parca Morta."

"You're no better than she is."

The twins sneered at her as well, as if only barely containing a laugh.

Claudia said nothing, merely shrugging her shoulders.

"Ha-ha! You two have a way of getting along with people!" Cecily broke in, pushing past them. "But I have to admit, I'm interested in taking on the Glühen Rose, too." She chuckled.

"Raigeki Senka… I don't think we've met."

"That's true. I've just been looking forward to a chance to meet such a powerful Strega in the arena," Cecily said, placing her hands on her hips. "Compared to you Dantes and Stregas, people pretty much think of us *daoshi* as having versatility at the expense of mastery. So it's always been a dream of mine to take down a top-class Strega like yourself in combat."

"Oh? I'll take that as a compliment."

The locked gazes of Julis and Cecily practically gave off sparks.

"E-everyone's really getting carried away...," Kirin whispered, watching the exchange from the sidelines.

"I guess there's no harm in having a bit of spirit, though," Ayato murmured back before realizing that someone on the opposing team was also watching on in silence.

Xiaohui Wu—the Celestial Warrior, Hagun Seikun.

His imperturbable demeanor showed not even a hint of the fervor that had engulfed his companions, quite as if it was his natural pose. Yet, despite that, he betrayed no sign of vulnerability or weakness.

"It looks like this is going to be just as difficult as I feared..."

"...Yes," Kirin murmured.

At that moment, Xiaohui's gaze turned toward them both.

"..."

He said nothing, nor did his eyes seem to convey anything. It was as if he was merely looking at them because they were there.

What in the...? Ayato thought.

He couldn't help but feel a sense of unease at that simple and unaffected expression. Those eyes were different than those of everyone he had fought thus far.

"Ayato... There's something strange about him..." Kirin, having noticed it, too, glanced sideways at him uneasily.

But before Ayato could put his finger on the source of that discomfort, Mico's excited voice echoed throughout the arena to announce the beginning of the match.

*

"Let's get this show started!" Cecily wasted no time before pulling out a spell charm. "*Jí jí rú lǜ lìng, chì!*" she cried, making a symbol with her first two fingers extended.

A tremendous roar engulfed the stage, with countless bolts of lightning crashing down like raindrops in a gale.

The world was dyed white by the flashes, the air filled with the scent of something burning.

"Another fancy introduction, I see…," Ayato murmured as he dodged the oncoming lightning and sped across the stage toward the silhouette in the rear of the opposing team's formation—Xiaohui Wu.

Cecily's particular *seisenjutsu* certainly lived up to her name: the Flower of a Thousand Thunderbolts, Raigeki Senka. That last technique, however, covered a wide area, and her aim, it seemed, wasn't precise.

"I don't think so!" Hufeng cried, leaping through the air with no concern for the lightning bolts crashing down around him.

How can he be so fast?!

Ayato swung the Ser Veresta in front of him. He had timed his countermove perfectly, completely in time with Hufeng's movements.

And yet, before it could make contact, Hufeng rebounded through the air as if kicking off an unseen wall, circling around to Ayato's rear.

The Tongtianzu…!

Ayato might also have had an Orga Lux, but that didn't mean he could respond to his opponent immediately. And to make matters worse, Hufeng was probably the fastest fighter in all of Asterisk.

"Ayato!" Kirin called out, placing herself between the two with her sword drawn.

"Agh—!"

"…*Boom*."

At the same moment, several bursts from Saya's Waldenholt Mark II homing blaster shot across the stage, arcing through the air as they descended upon their target.

Hufeng finally relented, clicking his tongue in annoyance as he pulled back.

"Kirin, now…!"

"Yes!"

Their first task was to break through the opposing team's formation.

In the center of the melee stood Xiaohui, waiting patiently, it seemed, for the two of them to engage.

Ayato and Kirin exchanged a brief look before descending upon their target from either side.

Xiaohui wasn't the kind of opponent to keep a hidden move in reserve, and they might not have another chance to close in on him simultaneously.

However—

"Wha—?!"

"Argh...!"

Xiaohui used his staff to repel the full force of both attacks—without, it seemed, so much as breaking a sweat.

It wasn't so much that he had parried both attacks practically at the exact same moment, but the fact that he had parried the Ser Veresta with nothing but a simple staff shook Ayato to his core.

"Impossible! Only another Orga Lux should be able to do that...!" Kirin exclaimed, her eyes wide in shock.

Only then did they realize that Xiaohui's staff—or rather, something coiling around his staff—seemed to be burning with a strange glow. It faded away after only a brief moment, but those few seconds were enough for Ayato to understand what had happened.

"A spell charm..."

"...Indeed. A charm for capturing your attacks and for releasing them—like this."

As far as Ayato was aware, this was the first time that Xiaohui had said anything to any of his opponents.

He had no time to dwell on that, however, as Xiaohui's counterattack soon appeared at either side.

"Watch out...!"

Ayato and Kirin leaped out of the way, and at that instant, the ground upon which they had been standing was blown away with a tremendous explosion. The power of the attack was nothing short of incredible.

"These charms have been placed on my staff many times over. No matter how many times you try, your Ser Veresta will never cut through."

"I see…"

In other words, the spell had absorbed the force of their joint attack and thrown it back at them.

In that case, the Ser Veresta ought to be able to cut through that counterattack.

Ayato still couldn't say that he had mastered the Orga Lux, but it should be able to withstand that much.

Just how many charms has he put on it, though…?

When he had fought the Li twins during the Phoenix, they'd had a seemingly limitless supply of spell charms at their disposal. Xiaohui would hardly be less well equipped than them.

"Now then…" Xiaohui raised his staff to face Ayato. "It's time for me to quench my master's thirst. Be ready."

Master? Does he mean Xinglou…?

There seemed to be some kind of hidden meaning behind those words, but now wasn't the time to dwell on them.

The next instant, Xiaohui's staff appeared before his eyes. Ayato managed to dodge it at the last possible moment, with Kirin taking advantage of that opportunity to circle around and attack their opponent from his right. Xiaohui, however, repelled her attack with his staff without so much as glancing toward her. Kirin tried to set herself up to use her Conjoined Cranes technique, but with a slight movement of his lips, Xiaohui sent the ground beneath her crumbling, and she lost her footing. "Wha—?!"

It looked like his charms were indeed some form of *seisenjutsu*.

Kirin had been distracted for only a brief moment, but Xiaohui had taken advantage of that opening to lash out with a powerful kick.

"*A-argh…!*"

She shielded herself with the Senbakiri, but the strike was enough to send her hurling across the stage. Xiaohui, on the other hand, used his staff to rebound off the ground and spin through the air, dodging Ayato's upward slash and countering downward with all the force of a hurricane.

Ayato was forced to take a step backward.

Before the staff could reach the ground, however, its trajectory quickly changed. Ayato tried to correct his footing, raising the Ser Veresta to his eyes to meet the attack, when—

"Oops…!"

Xiaohui lashed out, landing a flurry of consecutive punches right into the middle of his abdomen.

"—!"

Ayato had tried to focus his prana to withstand it, but the attack was so overpowering that it cut right through. So much air had been pushed out of his lungs that he couldn't even let out so much as a groan—but he managed, despite the pain, to force himself to roll away from his opponent and bring himself to his feet.

"*Urghk… Hghn…!*"

He fought to get his breathing under control. It was Kirin who had given him the chance to do so, standing ready at Xiaohui's rear and preventing him from following through with another attack. But even so—

"Hah… I think we're in trouble."

Xiaohui's abilities went far beyond their expectations.

He surpassed them both: in strength, technique, speed—everything. In both offense and defense, his movements totally eclipsed their own.

"*Wh-what do we have here?! Contestant Wu is overpowering Seidoukan's former and current number ones single-handed!*"

"*Hmm. He's a strong one, that's for sure.*"

As Mico's and Shizuna's voices filled the arena, Xiaohui quietly readied his staff.

Ayato wiped a streak of blood from his lips before flashing his opponent a forced grin as he raised the Ser Veresta in front of him.

In that case, there was only one thing left to do.

*

"You live up to your reputation, Glühen Rose!"

"Rgh…!"

A bolt of lightning lashed through the air, hurtling toward her.

Julis sacrificed one of the Livingston Daisies that she had already deployed to shield herself as she tried desperately to gather her scattered Rect Luxes.

All of a sudden, Saya's voice rang out: "Julis, above!"

"!"

At that moment, Hufeng came hurtling down with an ax kick.

"*Pēn!*"

Thankfully, she managed to dodge, but Hufeng quickly moved on to a series of consecutive kicks and elbow strikes, flowing from one to the next so quickly that Julis didn't even have a chance to catch her breath.

She managed to withstand the barrage thanks to the three Rect Lux units she had brought back under control, but that didn't change the fact that the situation was going from bad to worse.

Her opponent was simply too fast; even just defending herself required all her concentration. While she was able to use her Rect Lux through thought alone, that also meant that controlling it was a delicate affair, and all it would take was a lapse in concentration to find herself at a disadvantage.

If she was being honest with herself, she had to admit that the fact that she was able to keep up with him even this far was thanks to her intense training over the past year. Without that improvement, she would have had no hope of standing her ground.

"…Now!"

Saya released a barrage with her homing blaster to assist her, but before the beams could reach their target, a wall of lightning bolts crashed down to block them. Lasers and lightning alike collided in a violent flash, canceling each other out in a huge explosion.

"Stay out of this, kid!"

"Argh… Don't think you can talk down to me just because yours are bigger…! Stupid breasts!"

"…I wasn't talking about *that*."

Saya's oversized weapons required charging before every shot, so they had little chance of matching Cecily in speed. The rate at which she could use her spell charms was nothing short of incredible.

"...I guess I've got no choice."

Saya seemed to have realized that, too, as she quickly returned the Waldenholt to its activator and readied the Ark Van Ders Mark II.

Among her impressive arsenal, the Ark Van Ders was the most suitable for close combat—which basically meant it could be fired while still charging. Given the situation, that was no doubt her best option.

"You'd better not let down your guard around me...!"

Julis had been distracted for only a moment, but Hufeng had taken advantage of that to increase the intensity of his assault.

Julis's close-combat abilities were no match for those of her opponent. Her Rect Lux helped to compensate for that somewhat, but Hufeng had already batted away two of the three units she still had under her control.

She blocked an oncoming kick with the Nova Spina—used to control the other units of the Rect Lux—while using the last remaining unit to lash out at her opponent's fist. The next moment, however, he used all his strength to shatter the ground around them, blasting Julis aside before she even had a chance to react.

"*Ugh...*"

She winced at the pain, but fortunately, it was her left arm that was injured. Even if it was broken, she could still keep fighting. She gritted her teeth, preparing to meet another of his strikes, when she felt a cold shiver run down her spine.

The ground at her feet began to shimmer as a trap activated around her.

The Li twins...!

They must have used their illusion *seisenjutsu* to hide the spell charm.

A flurry of chains burst up from the ground, coiling around her body.

"This is it!" Hufeng cried out, lunging toward her exposed school crest, when—

"Sorry, Hufeng!" Cecily called out.

"—?!"

Saya, having escaped from Cecily's lightning bombardment, brought the Ark Van Ders down on Hufeng.

Hufeng began to cross his arms in an attempt to withstand the bombardment, but before he could properly ready himself, Saya pulled the trigger.

"Boom."

There was no hope of avoiding it at that range—or, at least, there shouldn't have been.

But Hufeng seemed to have pulled away just in time; he was simply there one moment and gone the next, as if he had somehow teleported out of the way.

"Heh…" Glancing at the burnt edges of his uniform, Hufeng let out a sigh of relief.

Julis, meanwhile, had used that opportunity to recall the units of her Rect Lux and break free.

"Thanks," she said, glancing toward Saya.

"Don't worry about it. I didn't think he'd be able to dodge it, though," she replied, her tone filled with a mixture of surprise and frustration.

It looked like she, too, had failed to appreciate just how fast Hufeng could move. Saya's eyesight had always been sharper than her own, so Julis had hoped that she, at least, would be able to keep pace with him. Thanks to the Tongtianzu, however, he was even faster than usual—too fast for even her to follow.

Hufeng, having rejoined Cecily, was discussing something with her in a hushed voice.

"I needed a breather, but what more can we do…?"

Their opponents were more formidable than any they had yet to face. Julis was supposed to be the team's raider, and Saya their rearguard, the two supporting Ayato and Kirin, but neither had any opportunity to come to their aid.

"Still, we can't give up," Saya murmured, as if reading her mind.

"...Right," Julis replied with a deep nod, tightening her grip on the Nova Spina.

*

"Heh-heh... It looks like we—"

"—have the superior team."

Claudia's battle against the twins was, compared to the others, somewhat less flashy.

"When the Glühen Rose stepped into my little trap—"

"—wasn't that your fault, Parca Morta?"

The twins appeared to be chuckling as they bolted across the stage, always maintaining a fixed distance from her, but Claudia, not allowing herself to be deceived, focused on her surroundings while attempting to discern their true locations.

At times, their figures seemed to melt away into thin air, or else multiply in front of her, but Claudia nonetheless continued to focus on their actual positions, trying to limit their opportunities to deceive or attack.

What she was doing wasn't as accurate as Ayato's *shiki* technique, but against opponents of this level—and given that she gave it all her concentration—she was able to make out their whereabouts fairly accurately. If she had been facing either of the twins one-to-one, she would have easily come out on top—but just as she had when Julis had been ensnared by that trap, she found herself slipping up when facing them both together.

Which was why she was using herself as bait to try to keep the two occupied.

But isn't that a tacit confession that I don't have any other options? In that case, I had better go all out.

The twins, no doubt, wanted to support their teammates. However, they couldn't afford to ignore the opponent in front them. They might have been able to do it if one of them was willing to sacrifice themselves, but if they did that in a team battle, they would end up losing their power balance.

Moreover, their opponent was the other side's team leader. If they were able to find an opening and destroy her school crest, that would be the end of the match. If they planned it properly, it wouldn't be impossible for them to snatch victory by themselves—and for them, there could be no more enticing prospect than that.

Claudia and the twins knew everything that they needed to know about one another, certainly enough to keep one another in check.

She knew, however, that she wouldn't be able to completely hold them down by herself.

Like the spell that had ensnared Julis earlier, the twins were succeeding in spreading the seeds of traps throughout the arena. There was nothing she could do about that.

"Hmm… You're certainly doing well, keeping us tied up all by yourself."

"Are you used to being chased, perhaps?"

"It must be tiring. All it would take is one oversight, and your friends would be finished."

"But no, we're going to stay here and take you down ourselves…"

The twins were doing everything in their power to whittle down her concentration.

If she could maintain the present state of affairs, victory would be hers.

However, if she slipped up, even if only for an instant, that would be the end for her.

She was walking a most precarious tightrope, with no option but to persevere.

Right. Even if the rest of her team were defeated, as long as she was still standing, the match wasn't over. There might come an opportunity to do something, but with the Pan-Dora's stock being what it was, she couldn't afford to act rashly…

At that moment—

"Are you thinking about something?" came Shenyun, appearing in front of her from out of nowhere.

"That won't do. You need to pay attention!" added Shenhua, quivering like a ghost before disappearing.

"*Ngh!*"

Shenyun had managed to worm his way inside her guard, lashing out with his elbow, and while Claudia managed to evade the attack, he followed through with a rapid succession of punches.

In this kind of close-combat fighting, the twins' martial arts were much more effective than her two swords.

"Did you think we'd just been fooling around this past year?" he gloated.

"We've been training, too, you know!" Shenhua's voice added from behind her.

"*Bào!*"

With that, she was engulfed in a violent explosion.

…Or so it had seemed.

"You certainly do look to have improved since the Phoenix…," Claudia said with a smile, having used the Pan-Dora to see through the illusion.

It was the same kind of spell charm that the twins had used against Ayato and Julis during their tag match—and surprisingly realistic when experienced firsthand.

"I see, so that was the Pan-Dora."

"What a nuisance."

The twins practically spat out the words.

If not for the Pan-Dora's precognition, she would have been in serious jeopardy. Perhaps the twins were stronger than she had suspected.

"Not to worry…"

"We've got plenty of time…"

The twins flashed her a pair of devilish grins before, once again, taking off down the stage.

Exactly. We still have time.

They would just have to carry out this contest of endurance all the way till its end, she thought as she took off in pursuit.

CHAPTER 3
THE CELESTIAL WARRIOR AND THE KEEN-EDGED TEMPEST

On that day, Xiaohui had been on the verge of death.

Indeed, had he passed even one more minute in that state, he very well might have died then and there at the age of only six years old.

The ruins of dilapidated towns and villages lined the barren remnants of what was once the Qingyi River. It was in the middle of the main road in one such settlement that Xiaohui lay, flat on his back, parched and unable to move.

"Oh… You have a good sacrum, boy," a voice said.

A woman wearing a strangely amicable smile had suddenly appeared within his vision. Everything looked yellow and blurred due to hunger and thirst, and so only her cheerful voice reached him clearly—distinct but, at the same time, strangely distant.

"Become mine. It would be a shame to let such raw talent go to waste. Although, if that *is* what you desire, I won't compel you otherwise…"

Xiaohui tried to respond, but he couldn't even produce so much as a weak groan. He succeeded only in opening his cracked lips a fraction wider.

"Don't fret. Just say it in your heart," the woman said, her voice remaining calm and detached.

And Xiaohui filled his mind with a single thought: *I don't want to die.*

At that moment, a lone tear dripped down his cheek.

"Very well. From now on, you belong to me," the woman said with a gentle smile before lifting a bamboo canteen to his lips.

The cold water flowed down his throat, and Xiaohui lost consciousness.

A world controlled by the integrated enterprise foundations required by simple necessity an underprivileged class. That wasn't to say that those on the other end of the spectrum lived in security and peace of mind. All it took was one mistake to be mercilessly cast down into the abyss.

Xiaohui's had been one such family, brought to ruin by some trivial blunder and scattered in the wind. While he was still too young to fully understand what was going on around him, his mother had taken him across the country, from one dilapidated provincial town to the next, until at last she, who had lived her whole life in luxury, could endure the hardship no longer and departed from the world, leaving him to fend for himself.

After an unknown time had passed, the young Xiaohui found himself wandering away from her cold sickbed, wandering without purpose or destination, until he could wander no longer.

"...!"

When he opened his eyes, he found himself in what looked like an old, elegant hermitage. Apart from the bed on which he was lying, the room was fitted only with a lacquered black desk. Even so, it looked to be meticulously maintained, unmarred by even a speck of dust.

He lifted himself up, glancing toward the latticed window at his side. Before him, he could see flowers rich in bloom, small birds singing, and a gentle light that glowed with all the colors of the rainbow. At the time, he had thought he must have died and woken up in paradise.

"Hmm, so you're awake. These drugs are strong, but you must be stronger still."

He glanced around, to find a woman standing at the foot of the bed.

She had long black hair, her modest clothes loose around her body. To his surprise, she was young—more girl than woman.

"...Where am I?"

"My hermitage at Huangshan. This area is filled with Nüwa stones—what you would call urm-manadite. They used to be quite useful, but I haven't touched them since I went to Emeishan."

For a brief second, Xiaohui wondered whether this kind of place could really exist, but he quickly cast aside his doubts. He knew instinctively that the normal rules of nature didn't apply to the woman standing in front of him.

"In this body, I go by the name of Xiaoyuan Wang. What are you called?"

Without waiting for him to respond, Xiaoyuan leaped, bringing her face up to his own. Her eyes stared into his, sucking him in, consuming his heart—his very soul.

"...Xiaohui Wu," he answered, his mouth moving of its own accord.

"Good. Well, Xiaohui. Do you remember agreeing to become mine?"

Xiaohui nodded.

At this, Xiaoyuan, too, nodded in satisfaction, her eyes narrowing in delight. "Good, good. Then let's start by hearing what you can do."

"What I can do...?" Xiaohui repeated, his mind going blank.

He ought to have been able to do whatever he wanted—not because his life had been saved, but because he himself wanted to do it.

That said, his six-year-old self had yet to fully comprehend that fact.

"...Tea..."

"Hmm?"

"I can make tea."

Desperately trying to call something to mind, those were the only words that came to his lips.

He had learned it from his mother and remembered fondly how

his parents had praised him after his first attempt. Since then, he had volunteered to brew the tea himself at every possible opportunity.

"Oh-ho! I see, I see. I'll have you make some later, then," Xiaoyuan said with a sonorous laugh, placing a hand on his head. "But, Xiaohui, that isn't all that I want from you. I need you to be strong."

"Strong…?"

"Indeed. Do you know any martial arts?"

Xiaohui shook his head.

He was a Genestella, but his mother had always detested fighting, and so he had never had an opportunity to learn anything like that.

"Hmm, very well. In that case, we'll have to start from the beginning. I will make you stronger, Xiaohui. Stronger, stronger, stronger, until one day you will be even stronger than I am… Satisfy me. That's all I wish from you." Xiaoyuan's eyes glowed like those of a child.

That was when Xiaohui first realized it, that the Xiaoyuan standing before him now, the young child that he saw in her eyes—this was her true self.

"…I'll do it. I promise," he answered, staring back into those warm, innocent eyes.

"A fine response… You should know, the signs all point to something great happening afar in the near future. I want to see it for myself. Which means that soon…yes, in four or five years, I will have to take a new body. You will need to grow during that time, too."

Xiaohui had no idea what she was talking about, but he nodded along regardless. He didn't want to disappoint her.

Xiaoyuan smiled down at him gently, stroking his head once more. "Well then, how about you brew that tea for me?"

Xiaohui's daily training regimen began that very day.

"Listen well, Xiaohui. The basic principle of this world is conflict. None of us can escape it. So we must master the art of war to give meaning to that conflict."

They began by training his body, building upon that foundation by learning new techniques little by little.

Xiaohui, who had no experience in the martial arts, devoured Xiaoyuan's teachings like cotton absorbs water.

That wasn't to suggest that the lessons were easy.

He would run through the untamed mountain, climb its sheer peaks, fight against Xiaoyuan with all his might, while she effortlessly resisted him using nothing but a single finger. When his body became worn out and exhausted, he would soak in the medicinal hot springs, the pain of his injuries searing through his body, tormenting him until the break of dawn.

And yet, he didn't once find those days to be unbearable, not even for a moment.

"Listen well, Xiaohui. It is knowledge that lies at the heart of martial arts, and knowledge is based on understanding."

It wasn't just the martial arts that Xiaoyuan taught him, but all of her accumulated wisdom.

Everything from arithmetic, to the motions of the stars, to how to communicate in various languages spoken all throughout the world, until Xiaohui came to wonder whether there wasn't anything that his master didn't know.

And sometimes, Xinglou would tell him about existences that defied the laws of nature.

"…Are you saying that there are other people like you out there?"

"Indeed. Well, I haven't seen them for a long time. In fact, I could count those with whom I still have contact on one hand." Xiaoyuan laughed nostalgically as she prepared an elixir by his bedside.

Xiaohui, in the center of that weak patch of candlelight, listened carefully to her gentle voice.

"I suppose the last time I met one of them in person was when I visited that decrepit old fool holed up in his ivory tower off in Europe. That must have been half a century ago now."

"Is there anyone else around here?"

"Well, now… There were quite a few sages here when I first came to this mountain… Unfortunately, we didn't get along."

"You didn't get along…? What do you mean?"

"They had thrown away their attachments. A rather tedious

bunch. The ability to laugh with joy, to writhe in agony, to cry in despair—they had practically given up on life itself. Don't you make the same mistake. A good sacrum is said to be proof of great talents, but it's you who needs to clear your own path forward."

"I see..."

By then, Xiaohui was already half asleep and couldn't make out the bitter smile that had appeared on Xiaoyuan's face.

Several years passed, and Xiaohui found himself gradually becoming able to hold his own as Xiaoyuan's sparring partner. Even she was astonished by his progress—and by the fact that he had managed to pick up *seisenjutsu* almost immediately.

"You're even more talented than I had imaged," she exclaimed after one of their training sessions, her pleasure shining through. She was sitting cross-legged on the floor of their training room, a cup of her student's tea in her hand.

"...I'm honored," Xiaohui responded graciously, his voice ringing with confidence.

"Hmm... It's a shame that that charm of yours has all but disappeared, though. Whatever happened to your cute nature?" Xiaoyuan asked, catching him in a sudden embrace.

"M-master!" Xiaohui exclaimed, his cheeks turning red as he looked away. "Please, stop playing around...!"

"Oh-ho, I see. So there's still something left in there." For a short moment, she knuckled her student on the head before suddenly letting go and returning to her usual serious expression. "Now then, you should be able to fend for yourself now. The time has come for me to take on a new body."

"Master...?"

"I will return here in a few years' time. Until then, you must continue your training by yourself," Xiaoyuan said, her voice solemn, before holding out a sealed scroll.

"...Very well," answered Xiaohui, carefully taking it in his hands.

Xiaoyuan gave him a satisfied nod, though her expression still contained a touch of unease.

*　　*　　*

Xiaohui maintained his daily regimen, training in solitary silence for the next six years.

He polished his techniques as per the instructions Xiaoyuan had left him, focusing day after day on improving himself for the time when his master would finally return.

All the while, he kept what she had said to him close to heart.

Yes, he would become stronger.

Stronger than he was now, stronger even than Xiaoyuan herself. Because that was what she wanted of him.

Before long, he found himself having grown taller than he remembered her being herself, having grown, to anyone who might have seen him, into a tall young man who showed no resemblance whatsoever to the boy who had once been hanging on the verge of death in the middle of a deserted road.

And then, while meditating deep inside the hermitage, he heard the high-pitched sound of a door creaking open.

Amid the spring light that flooded the room was a small silhouette.

Xiaohui, quite as if he had known she was coming, immediately fell to his knees, head bowed.

"Welcome back, master."

"Oh-ho-ho! You've grown since I last saw you, my dear student."

The laughter that greeted him was different than he remembered, the innocent, childish figure before him that of someone else.

But there could be no mistaking that it was her.

"Now then, get ready. We're going to Rikka."

"Yes, master."

Xiaohui had begun his preparations as instructed when the young girl clapped her hands together, just like he remembered. "Ah, yes. I forgot to mention it. My name now is Xinglou. Xinglou Fan."

*

"Haaa!"

Xiaohui brushed aside Ayato's downward stroke of the Ser Veresta with his staff, at the same time twisting his body to dodge Kirin's oncoming attack from his right.

Her katana continued its arc, however, carving through the air as it zeroed in on his chest. At the same time, Ayato, having regained his balance, thrust the Ser Veresta straight at him.

Xiaohui, holding his staff one-handed, parried the oncoming strike while using his free hand to brush aside Kirin's Senbakiri. One of the charms wrapped around his staff quickly burned itself out, pushing Ayato backward with tremendous force while he spun around to take down Kirin—who only just managed to jump to safety at the last moment.

His two opponents put some distance between themselves and him. Xiaohui returned to his usual stance.

As could have been expected from Seidoukan's current and former number ones, they were both of consummate skill and ability. Battling them both at the same time—all it would take was a single mistake, and he might end up losing his school crest.

But of course, there was no chance of that happening. Xiaohui had long since resolved to dedicate everything he had to his master, Xinglou.

His heart, his prowess at martial arts, his techniques, his words—everything he had, his life included, he had dedicated to her.

To repay her, to grant her wish.

Which was why he would never make a mistake.

"*Jí jí rú lǜ lìng, chì!*" he chanted as he made the symbol with his fingers, when a wall of fire erupted in front of his opponents.

Ayato didn't hesitate to cut through it with the Ser Veresta, but by then, Xiaohui had already moved into his blind spot.

Xiaohui was well aware that Xinglou wasn't satisfied with his current level of skill, so he had no idea whether she was enjoying what she saw that day.

In the end, it was up to her. It wasn't something for him to know.

So he just had to do what he always did—fight as best he could, without holding anything back.

"*Pò!*"

"Oh, crap!"

Ayato had noticed the oncoming attack, but Xiaohui was still faster.

There was no opening to reach his school crest, but Xiaohui landed three consecutive blows along the right-hand side of his body: on his shoulder, chest, and thigh.

"Ugh...!"

Ayato fell to his knees, finally giving Xiaohui an opening for his prize.

First, he would take down this one.

He lashed out with an assured blow—only to have Kirin's Senba-kiri appear in front of him.

"I won't let you!" she shouted.

"...!"

Xiaohui's brow wrinkled slightly. He hadn't let down his guard against her; on the contrary, he had judged that she wouldn't make it there in time.

Did I misread her...? No, but then...

Kirin was staring straight at him. Had he simply imagined the strange glint in her eyes?

He took a half step back, when—

"Sorry, Elder Brother! You might want to look away!"

A blinding burst and a terrible roar engulfed the stage as a torrent of lightning came crashing down.

*

"There's no need to go crazy on my account, Raigeki Senka!" Julis bellowed.

"Ha-ha-ha-ha! What, is this too much for you?" Cecily laughed back.

Lightning continued to tear into the stage from every angle, cutting through the air like countless soaring dragons.

The storm she had unleashed at the beginning of the match had been like an out-of-control tempest, but this was at a completely different level.

Dodging those blasts of electricity had become much more difficult, as not only were they crashing down from above, but now they
also ran practically parallel to the ground. It was an attack directed
not at specific targets, but at specific trajectories—although, luck-
ily, their distribution seemed to be randomized. Nonetheless, Julis
knew she'd have to keep an eye on it.

"*Ngh!* Fine, let's do this properly, then!" Julis cried out as she
thrust her hands down onto the ground, summoning up an enor-
mous magic circle on the stage floor.

"Burst into bloom—*Grevillea!*"

With that, pillars of fire at least ten meters tall erupted out of the
ground throughout the arena, colliding with Cecily's lightning in a
massive explosion of mana.

In the center of that explosion, Ayato, Kirin, and Xiaohui had
resumed their contest.

And then—

"*Pò!*"

Saya emerged from the roiling flames, catching Hufeng's oncoming kick with the body of the Ark Van Ders.

"…Ugh!"

She shook off the heavy blow, but Hufeng leaped back into the air,
circling around her as if rebounding off unseen walls. His movements were fast—too fast to be seen with the naked eye.

His attacks could come from any direction, so it required everything
they had just to stay on alert. Nonetheless, her injuries were mounting.

"I'll show you no mercy!"

"…Ngh!"

Even so, Hufeng still had to avoid the lightning and flames that
now filled the arena, meaning that his movements were, at least,
partially restricted. If not for that, he might have already defeated
her. At the very least, she was no match for him at close quarters.

"Even so…!"

Saya poured her prana into the Ark Van Ders, waiting for a chance
at a Hail Mary strike.

She had made contact with him just before, but so far, he had managed to evade most of her attacks. If she didn't time it right, it would be practically impossible to hit her target.

Just as she was trying to line up a shot, Hufeng made his most daring leap yet, landing directly in front of her.

"—!"

"I've got you now!"

Saya quickly lowered her weapon to catch him, but Hufeng swiftly brushed it aside and drove his elbow into the pit of her stomach.

"Gah…!"

His fist came flying toward her school crest, but she managed to twist away just before it could make contact.

However, as if having anticipated this move, Hufeng then swept her feet out from under her. But Saya sunk her weapon into the ground and used it as a pivot to swing to safety.

Hufeng leaped after her as she again lined up her shot, but it was too late. This was the chance she had been waiting for.

"Now!"

She swung the Ark over her shoulder, tightening her hold on its grip, and pulled the trigger just as Hufeng was about to dash toward her once more. She hadn't had much time to aim, but at this range, there was no way she could miss.

The burst of light made a direct hit on its target—and went right through.

"Wha—?!"

For a second, Hufeng's figure seemed to waver in the air before disappearing like a mirage.

An illusion?!

But by the time she realized what had happened, it was already too late.

"I didn't want to have to rely on those twins to do this… My apologies!" came a voice from her rear, when something collided into her with a tremendous impact, like a giant boulder falling down and crushing her underneath. Everything went black.

*   *   *

"Saya Sasamiya—unconscious."

"Saya…!" Julis hissed at the sound of the automated voice before turning back to her own opponent. "Damn it! You can't keep this up forever!"

"Oh? And why not?" responded Cecily as she pursued her across the battlefield, surrounded by countless saber-like lightning bolts.

Each one was powerful enough to tear a hole through the base of the stage, but with their user's aim being what it was, dodging them wasn't too difficult.

Nonetheless, now that Saya wasn't tying Hufeng down, she had no more time to waste.

"Because I won't let you! Burst into bloom—*Antirrhinum Majus!*"

She drew an outline of a magic circle with the Nova Spina, from which burst the figure of a fire-clad dragon.

"Heh, so it's tiger versus dragon, is it?" Cecily had taken a bunch of spell charms in one hand, using the other to make a series of unusual gestures.

"Jí jí rú lǜ lìng, chì!"

The charms activated in a cloud of lightning, writhing in the air as if a living thing, until, just as Cecily had said, it had vaguely taken on the form of a tiger.

"Let's see whose is the strongest!"

Both elemental creatures were close to equal in size—but Julis, her face grave, wasn't going to just watch from the sidelines.

"I'll crush you!" she cried out, recalling six of her fallen Rect Lux units and positioning them around the dragon.

"Bloom!"

At that moment, the Lux blades flew through the air as the dragon swelled to almost three times its prior size.

"Wh-wha—?!"

The flames practically swallowed the tiger-shaped cloud of lightning whole before swooping down toward Cecily. A wave of panic spreading across her face, she continued to desperately cast more spell charms in rapid succession, summoning up a wall of lightning to protect herself—but the dragon simply opened its maw wider, engulfing them all in a powerful explosion.

Julis covered her face with her arms to shield herself from the heat of the blast.

She had synchronized the particular junction pattern of her mana and prana with the units of her Rect Lux to temporarily boost the power of the technique. It was only the second time she had managed to pull it off in the middle of battle, and the first time in conjunction with a move as destructive as the Antirrhinum Majus.

When the flames subsided, a motionless figure lay sprawled in the middle of a deep crater.

"Cecily Wong—crest broken."

"Ah-ha-ha... You got me," Cecily said with a bitter smile. "Argh, why did I go with *seisenjutsu*? I should have done this the old-fashioned way."

Cecily's martial arts certainly had been beyond compare during the Phoenix four years ago. If she had used those against her, Julis would no doubt have found herself in a difficult position.

But if she had done that, her team would have had inadequate support. It wasn't a one-on-one contest, so it made sense for her to take over the rearguard.

It looked like Cecily understood that, too. "Well, it's just me who's out, not the team. It isn't the end of the world..."

"—!"

Before she could finish, Julis leaped backward, and the ground where she had been standing suddenly erupted before her.

"Tenka Musou!"

It was indeed Hufeng on the other side of the roiling dust. She tried to brace herself with the Nova Spina, but she had already exhausted her prana with that last move.

I guess I still haven't really recovered from yesterday...

Of course, Hufeng hadn't failed to notice that, either.

The next moment, he descended upon her faster than the eye could see, carving straight through her crest.

"Julis-Alexia von Riessfeld—crest broken."

"Ayato, I can handle this! Go help Claudia!" Kirin called out over the automated voice announcing Julis's defeat as she parried Xiaohui's staff.

"But don't you…?"

It was obvious, now that both Julis and Saya had been eliminated, that Hufeng would go for their team leader. Even with the Pan-Dora, Claudia couldn't face three opponents alone.

He knew that she needed someone to back her up, but he couldn't just leave Kirin to face Xiaohui by herself. Even with the two taking him on together, he still had the upper hand.

"Don't worry. I've realized something."

"Huh…?"

"Trust me, Ayato! I'll be okay!"

"…All right."

He couldn't afford to waste time asking what exactly she meant. She seemed confident about it, whatever it was, so he had no choice but to trust her.

He got his breathing under control, focusing his attention on the other side of the stage, before rushing over to Claudia.

"Ayato!" Claudia's expression was one of relief as he appeared by her side.

That was understandable, given that she had been fighting alone thus far. Before they could say anything more, however, the air around them seemed to waver as Hufeng appeared behind them.

"Claudia, get down!"

But she had already begun to dive out of the way before he could finish speaking. She had probably used the Pan-Dora.

Ayato leaped over her, wincing slightly as a dull pain ran through his right leg, and then swept the Ser Veresta downward.

"*Jí!*"

To Ayato's surprise, Hufeng caught the attack with a kick—or more precisely, with the back of his outstretched leg.

Of course. Those armored boots were an Orga Lux.

"Why did you think I brought these out?" Hufeng called out as he swept the Ser Veresta aside. He twisted through the air, rushing toward him.

Ayato ducked down just as Hufeng vanished.

Instead, the twins now stood on either side of him, spell charms ready. But that wasn't Ayato's main concern. "Claudia, he's headed your way!"

"I know!" she called back.

Shenyun grimaced as he threw himself out of the path of Ayato's oncoming sword.

And then, the figures of the twins, lunging toward him to attack, simply melted away.

"That *shiki* of yours—"

"—is a real nuisance..."

Shenyun and Shenhua both glared at him resentfully.

Ayato poured his prana into his weapon, using Meteor Arts to mow down everything around him. Behind the brilliant afterimage, the traps that Shenhua had just set burned away unused.

"Thank you, Ayato!" Claudia said with a bright laugh, moving to stand back-to-back against him.

"There's probably still more of them out there, though, so keep your eyes open."

"Argh..." Shenhua glared at him, but Ayato had more immediate concerns.

Hufeng was speeding toward him once again.

"*Pò!*"

Ayato repulsed Hufeng's ax kick with his sword, forcing him back. Hufeng was quick to react, but it seemed he was being particularly vigilant around the Ser Veresta. At least to a certain extent, that made his movements easier to read.

"*Pēn!*"

Ayato dodged the downward strike, thrusting back at his opponent's chest. Hufeng managed to dodge the blade with only a hair's breadth to spare before leaping forward once more, lashing out with his elbow. Ayato, however, took ahold of that arm with his free hand, letting his prana flow through him as he flung his opponent backward—yet, it was Hufeng, bracing his legs against an invisible wall, who ended up launching Ayato across the stage.

"Ugh..."

It looked like Hufeng was indeed the stronger of the two when it came to unarmed combat. And of course, Ayato was still wounded from his earlier engagement with Xiaohui. The pain running through his shoulder continued unabated.

Even so, he managed to correct his bearing before he hit the ground and landed safely before readying himself to meet Hufeng's oncoming midair kick. His opponent leaped over him, unleashing a torrent of high-speed strikes. Ayato swung the Ser Veresta backward, meeting those blows head-on as his own weapon repeatedly collided with the Tongtianzu.

Brilliant sparks flew in every direction as the two Orga Luxes clashed against each other, until the two fighters' attacks became so powerful as to force both of them apart.

"I should have expected as much from the Murakumo..." Hufeng's breathing was ragged, but his smile was one of excitement. "You really are an outstanding opponent!"

"I could say the same about you!" Ayato replied, just as a strange feeling began to well up inside him.

It was the same dull throbbing in his chest that he had felt during the Gran Colosseo when he had witnessed Earnest's and Sylvia's abilities firsthand.

No, Ayato reminded himself, quashing the thought. *The team comes first...*

He edged closer to his opponent, keeping his gaze locked on Hufeng.

It was clear that Hufeng was focusing his prana into his legs. He was no doubt planning to leap forward with explosive force in an attempt to settle their duel.

The air practically throbbed with tension, until finally, it came to a head.

"——, *crest broken.*"

The mechanical voice rang coolly across the stage.

*

"...I see."

Watching Ayato rush to Claudia's aid out of the corner of her eye, Kirin held the Senbakiri at eye level as she faced off against Xiaohui.

Her opponent, staff held low, knees bent, wore a suspicious frown. "What are you up to?"

"What am I up to...? Do you mean, why did I tell Ayato to go?"

It was the first time that Xiaohui had said anything to her. Kirin, surprised, wanted to choose her words carefully, without allowing her concentration to lapse.

"You can't fight me alone."

There was no trace of conceit behind those words; he had uttered them merely as an objective fact.

"Maybe not. But still...I won't know unless I try!" Kirin cried as she leaped forward with an upward swing of her blade.

Xiaohui raised his staff to block the attack, while at the same time making a gesture with his free hand, summoning up a powerful gale that pushed her backward across the stage.

"*Ugh...!*"

This was it.

Under any normal circumstances, she would be able to flow from one strike to the next with the Toudou school's Conjoined Cranes technique, but that wasn't an option against Xiaohui. Put simply, he was too fast for her—the number of skills at his disposal too great.

There was little chance she would be able to take him down in this state.

"*Pò!*"

Using the powerful gale at his back to leap after her, Xiaohui lunged toward her school crest, but Kirin managed to evade the attack by running toward him herself. His staff still made contact with her cheek, but she couldn't afford to dwell on the blood that now dripped from the shallow cut.

Xiaohui's staff was sharp and heavy. If she tried to parry his attacks with it head-on, there was a high chance that it would end up breaking the Senbakiri.

"*Jí!*"

Even so, the normal strategies for dealing with an opponent armed with a long weapon wouldn't be effective against Xiaohui's martial arts. Indeed, just as she was thinking that, he immediately followed through with a charged punch with his free hand.

The attack, made all the more powerful by his having channeled his prana into it, could have ended up shattering her bones if she had met it head-on.

Instead, she twisted her body out of the way, dodging it at a hair's breadth. The strike grazed across her left shoulder, tearing her uniform and skin.

"Haaaaaaaaaaaaaaaa!"

She countered with a wide swing of the Senbakiri, its tip reaching within a few centimeters of her opponent's school crest—but by the time that it had gotten that far, Xiaohui, like she herself had done just before, had already spun out of its path.

He twisted through the air before lashing out with a backhanded punch aimed for her head.

Kirin, however, again ducked out of the way, leaving only a few strands of glittering silver hair to fall softly to the ground.

"Haaah...haaah..." Her breathing was growing ragged, but her concentration hadn't flagged.

She could still win.

"...How?" Xiaohui asked, the two opponents having retreated

from each other after their rapid exchange of blows. His gaze seemed to be filled with even greater suspicion than last time. "How did you dodge that attack? It would have been impossible for you just a moment ago."

"I'm not the same person I was a moment ago," Kirin replied firmly, leaping forward with a downward stroke of her blade.

In actual fact, not even she could say how exactly she had done it. She could just read him better than she could before. She could gauge his movements based on the way he concentrated his prana throughout his body. She wasn't lying when she had told Ayato that she had realized something.

She had always been unusually sensitive to the flow of prana. Any Genestella could discern the movements of another person's prana, but her understanding went to a deeper level in a way even she couldn't properly describe. It was thanks to that that she had been able to master the Conjoined Cranes at such a young age.

And this wasn't the first time she had been able to completely read an opponent through the way they focused their prana. However, whereas her previous experiences had lasted only for a short moment, she found herself now filled with a newfound confidence.

"The spirit of Tianshang Shengmu...?" Xiaohui murmured under his breath.

Kirin had no idea what he meant, but there was something else bothering her. "Do you mind if I ask a question of my own?" she asked, her gaze fixed on his face.

"What?"

"You... You aren't trying to win, are you?"

Xiaohui's eyes opened wide, as if caught off guard.

Right. That sense of unease that had been at the back of her mind since first facing off against him—it stemmed from his extreme selflessness.

"...Exactly. For me, victory is no more than a maximum display of one's own power against an opponent."

"In other words, you aren't bothered about the outcome?"

"Is there anything wrong with that?" Xiaohui responded calmly.

Kirin pursed her lips in mild annoyance, shaking her head. "No. As a warrior, that's…probably a very idealistic way of thinking. It's a wonderful thing to want to better yourself and to simply want to fight at your best, without worrying about whether you win or lose," Kirin said before catching her breath. "But I'm not so broad-minded… I want to win!"

"Then why do *you* seek victory? For yourself? For your friends? Or maybe you hope to win the tournament to have a wish granted?" As he spoke, Xiaohui was letting his prana flow through his body. He no doubt meant to bring their contest to an end.

Kirin, too, let her prana flow through her as she responded: "For all those things. I want to win for my own world!"

The two leaped toward each other.

Xiaohui's staff spun upward with a howl, cutting through the air as it approached. Kirin, however, had already taken account of his movements. But of course, while she could read those movements in advance, she couldn't hope to surpass him in terms of raw technique. If she wanted to beat him, there would only be one way to do it.

She stepped backward just far enough to dodge Xiaohui's low attack as he tried to knock her off her feet; steadied herself as she turned aside his next strike with the Senbakiri; then spun out of the way of what was meant to be a surprise hand-to-hand attack.

It was a fierce series of moves, leaving her without any chance to counter.

Even with the ability to read his actions in advance, she was at her limit just trying to keep up with him.

"*Jí jí rú lǜ lìng, chì!*" Xiaohui chanted as a surge of lightning exploded in front of her.

She shielded her eyes, but a sharp burning pain ran through her left arm. Because of the distraction, she had been too slow to react to Xiaohui's next strike with his staff. It had probably left her arm broken.

But she couldn't do anything about that now.

She shifted her hold on the Senbakiri to better control the weapon one-handed before lunging toward her opponent's school crest.

There was no way she could have missed, and yet, the strike simply passed straight through its target with no resistance. Xiaohui's figure wavered in the air for a second before disappearing.

An illusion?!

She had assumed that only the twins would use those, but there was no reason to have thought that Xiaohui wouldn't be able to do so, either. She cursed herself for not realizing it sooner.

"This is it…!" Xiaohui, taking full advantage of the opportunity, swept his staff toward her.

Having seen the oncoming blow out of the corner of her eye, she had just enough time to leap out of the way but ended up losing her balance and falling to her knees.

Xiaohui changed his trajectory, homing in on her school crest with the tip of his weapon.

Once more, however, Kirin saw that coming. Her eyes flashed with a purple glimmer as she watched him fill his body with prana and exhaust it all in a sudden move.

She raised the Senbakiri one-handed to defend herself. A clear, crystalline sound rang out as the katana shattered, but she wasted no time before rushing toward Xiaohui's chest.

Only the base of her blade remained, but that was enough.

Xiaohui was strong.

She still hadn't been able to land any real attacks against him. The difference in ability between the two was clear, and he wasn't the kind of fighter to let down his guard or underestimate his opponents.

Even so, Kirin didn't hesitate.

It was her need to win that kept her going. An unbecoming reason, but that was what it was.

She had seen what drove Ayato, Saya, Julis, and Claudia forward—she understood what they wanted, why they needed to win. All those things existed in her world, too; all of them gave her the power to keep going.

A wall of fire began to erupt in her path, but she had seen through that, too. It was the same technique that Xiaohui had used against Ayato earlier, and Kirin had made the connection between his

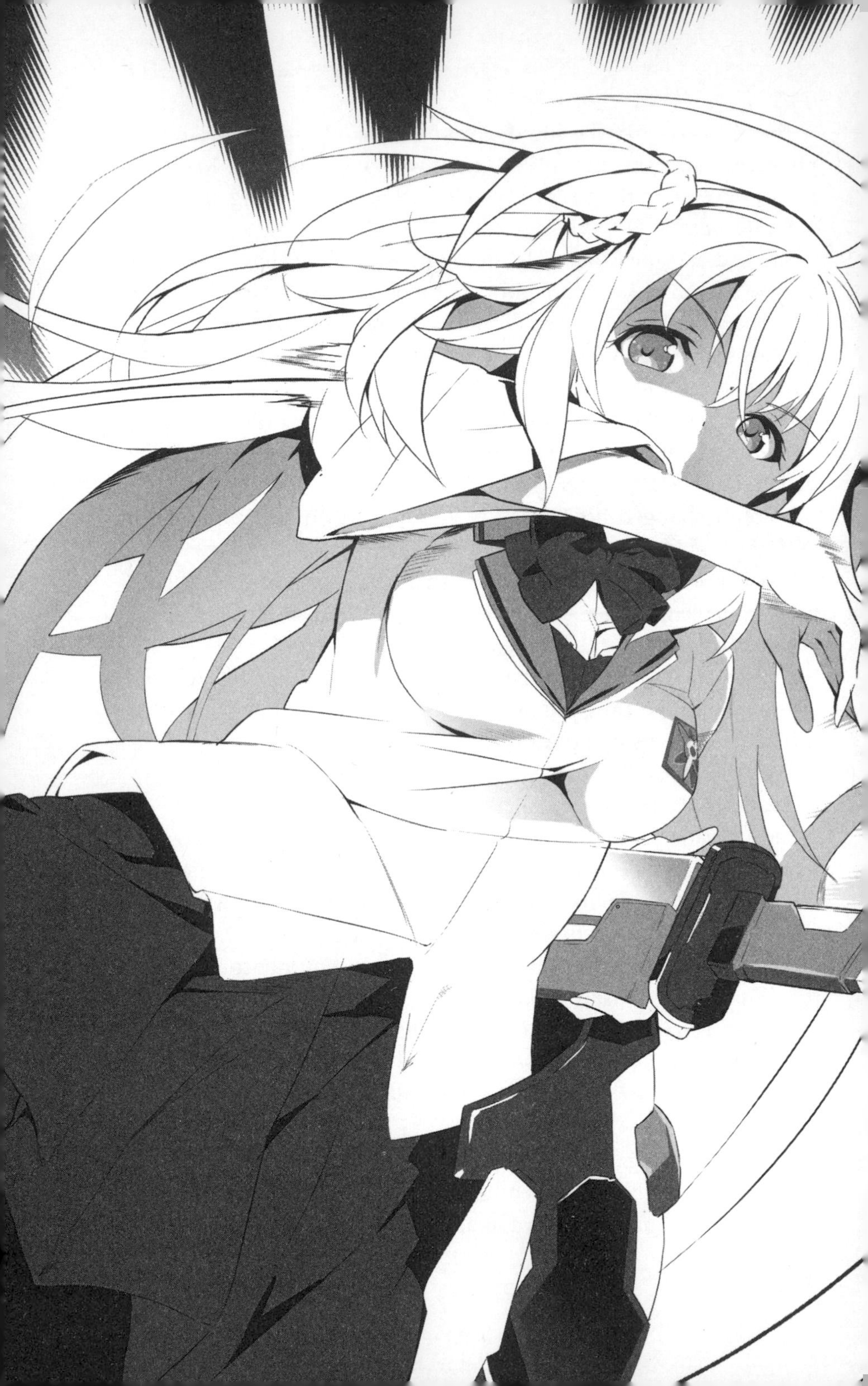

techniques and the symbols he made with his fingers, the movements of his lips.

Before the flames could fully emerge, she wrapped herself around her opponent's arm, guiding her broken sword toward his school crest.

For the first time, Xiaohui's eyes opened wide in shock.

Still, he didn't allow himself to falter. Letting his staff drop to the ground, he readied himself to meet her with his bare hands, one fist clutching a glowing spell charm.

"*Bào!*"

A huge conflagration engulfed half the stage, followed by a tremendous explosion of searing wind.

It was a merciless attack, and one that, at this range, would risk engulfing him, too—which meant he would have had to have positioned it perfectly.

In which case—

Kirin spun around behind him, her legs screaming with pain as she pushed herself beyond her physical capabilities.

Just a little longer...

"Aaaaaargh!" Xiaohui let out an earsplitting war cry as he prepared to meet her attack.

He let out his fastest punch yet—but Kirin, filled with admiration for her opponent, let it swing past her, thrusting what remained of the Senbakiri at his chest.

It was, when all was said and done, only a broken sword.

Yet, it still reached its target.

"Xiaohui Wu—crest broken."

Kirin's final movements, her series of offensive and defensive maneuvers that completely engulfed her opponent, were as graceful and elegant as the folding of an origami crane.

CHAPTER 4
CLAIRVOYANCE

"Did we…win?" Julis murmured, falling to her knees in disbelief.

When the protective gel surrounding the stage was deactivated, a deafening roar of cheers descended upon Ayato and the others, followed by the impassioned voices of the announcer and commentator.

"Th-that's it! What a conclusion! The winner is Seidoukan Academy's Team Enfield!"

"This certainly is an unexpected victory. To be perfectly honest, there should have been a significant difference in ability between Contestant Toudou and Contestant Wu, and yet…"

"…Elder Brother…" Hufeng, standing across from Ayato, looked as if he couldn't believe what had just happened.

"…"

Even so, judging by his expression, it was Xiaohui who was the most surprised of all.

"I… I lost… I see…"

Watching him murmur those brief words to himself, Ayato felt that he had seen Xiaohui exhibit something resembling honest emotion for the first time. It was a meager, fragmentary change, but there was unmistakably something different about him now compared to when he had first entered the stage.

At that moment, Kirin staggered weakly and lost her balance.

"Kirin!" Ayato rushed over to catch her just before she could hit the ground.

She seemed to be completely sapped of energy, but even so, she gave him a brave smile. "Th-thank you, Ayato... Did we...? Did we win?"

"Thanks to you!" Ayato beamed. "You were amazing, Kirin!"

But then he noticed something was wrong.

Her eyes were out of focus, her voice terribly weak.

"I—I see... Thank...goodness... But still... Why is everything... so...bright?"

"Kirin! Kirin!"

Just as she lost consciousness—

"Oh-ho, fret not."

The voice was by no means loud enough to bury the roar of the crowd. On the contrary, it was soft and childish, with a light, mellow ring.

Ayato turned toward it reflexively, to see a void in the center of the stage, as if the air itself had been ripped open. From it emerged the figure of a girl.

"Xinglou...!"

"...Huh? Huh? Whaaat? Wh-what's this? A child has appeared in the middle of the stage...!"

"Oh... It's the Ban'yuu Tenra..." Compared to Mico's flustered voice, Hiiragi's was a strange mix of resignation and curiosity.

"Th-the Ban'yuu Tenra?! Now that you mention it, that girl does look like Jie Long's number one, Xinglou Fan! Wh-why on earth could someone normally so reclusive enter the stage now...? No, no, before that—how did she enter the stage...?" Mico exclaimed, coming out with one question after another.

A commotion was beginning to ferment among the spectators, too.

Xinglou, however, paid them all no heed.

"She has looked into the vein of life," the girl—Xinglou—explained with a hint of admiration as she stared at Kirin's motionless face.

"The sight will have been burned into her eyes. She should return to normal within two or three days."

"The vein of life...?" Ayato repeated.

"Clairvoyance—the ability to read one's intentions, only discernible through their prana. She no doubt read Xiaohui's every move," Xinglou explained.

Ayato didn't understand. "You mean...like the Pan-Dora's precognition?"

"No." Xinglou shook her head. "That Orga Lux reveals the future of the world. That is what makes it such a powerful weapon for gathering information. No, what she saw isn't the future of the world, but just one's intentions. You could think of it more like mind reading."

"So she knew what he was going to do because it's what he *wanted*?"

"Exactly. She knew how he wanted to act," Xinglou said with a nod, her lips pursed. "It's a formidable natural talent. To think that she can do this much without proper training... To be honest, not even I suspected she would come this far. If someone like me was to recklessly come into contact with someone like her, overflowing with talent polished through her own efforts, I could end up breaking her. I intended to leave her alone until she had fully ripened, but now that she's here, I can hardly resist taking such a fragrant treat..."

"...I think I can say on her behalf that she isn't interested." Ayato tightened his grip on Kirin, narrowing his eyes at the child.

"I'm not fool enough to pluck a budding flower before it blooms."

"...More importantly, is she going to be okay?"

Kirin hadn't budged an inch since losing consciousness. Her breathing seemed to have come under control, but her complexion wasn't good, and she seemed completely sapped.

"Even with training, looking into the flow of life requires great exertion. This is what happens when you overdo it, as she did. Think of it like exhausting your prana. Her life isn't in danger, but it's no less serious than a physical injury. You should take her somewhere to recover."

"…Got it. Thank you, Xinglou."

In that case, it would be better to wait for the first-aid staff to come to them rather than try to move her himself.

Saya, it seemed, had lost consciousness as well and was being seen to by Claudia.

"…Master…"

The five members of Team Yellow Dragon had assembled behind Xinglou and were kneeling reverently.

"I'm truly sorry for this defeat," Xiaohui said as the team's representative, his head bowed.

"Oh-ho, I don't recall instructing you to win. What I wanted in exchange for teaching you was for you to satisfy me. You knew that."

"Even so…," Xiaohui began, his voice and face stiff.

Xinglou looked down at him with a joyful grin. "Oh-ho! Listen up, Xiaohui! This was my first time seeing that expression on you. Yes, it wasn't victory I wanted… But that's different from *you* not seeking victory." With that, she narrowed her eyes, a cool chill entering her voice. "You have a brilliant mind, Xiaohui. Whether it's martial arts or *seisenjutsu*, you absorb anything that comes your way. You're faithful to my teachings, and you've never opposed me. Yes, you're a truly excellent disciple. But unfortunately, I've no interest in doting on mere puppets."

"…"

Xiaohui listened on in silence, his gaze directed at the ground.

"Your techniques are mine—faithfully reproduced, yes, but not developed, not made your own. I suppose it's clear by now that you're not interested in moving beyond that point. You're only trying to satisfy me, only trying to meet my expectations. You don't do it for yourself. There's no satisfaction to be found in training with someone like that, someone who can't be tempered into something greater."

"Master…" Only now did Xiaohui move, tilting his head to stare up at Xinglou.

His face was like that of a child watching his mother bid farewell.

"Do you understand why I like your tea? Because that's the only thing that you've mastered for yourself, that you've studied for yourself, that you've cultivated for yourself."

At these words, Xiaohui's eyes opened wide.

"However, defeat is humiliating. That is for the best. Now you have a reason to want to free yourself from that which binds you."

"But, master! I—"

"I appreciate your loyalty, but you should be a person, not a doll," Xinglou interrupted with a gentle shake of her head. "If you won't do that, you'll never satisfy me."

"...Yes, master."

"Mm-hm." Xinglou nodded before turning her gaze back to Ayato. "Now I must express my gratitude to that girl—Kirin Toudou. She has my thanks for besting this one here. She fought splendidly."

"...I'll let her know when she wakes up."

"Good. As a matter of fact, if anyone was going to defeat him, I assumed it would be you. Maybe I need to wait a little longer?" Xinglou said with a suggestive smile, patting him on the shoulder.

"Huh?"

"I'm looking forward to the championship. Do make it an interesting one." With that, she let out a dry laugh, then led Team Yellow Dragon away.

Ayato let out a sigh of relief as, in their place, the first-aid staff made their way onto the stage.

*

In the student council president's office at Saint Gallardworth Academy—

"...So Team Enfield came out on top. Impressive, truly impressive," began Ernest Fairclough as he watched the post-match commentary on the air-window. "I suppose we should call this Miss Toudou's awakening? Although, I must admit, it was a little unexpected… Well then, what do you all say?" He turned to glance at the four other members of Team Lancelot, all gathered in the room.

"Heh-heh! It's just like I said, right? I told you they'd make it to the finals!" Laetitia declared as she brushed her hair back with a flourish.

She was no doubt overjoyed to have finally been given a chance to face off against her rival, Claudia. She was clearly trying to act calm and composed, but she couldn't hide the faint flush that had risen to her cheeks.

"We should welcome this outcome. It should work to our advantage. To be honest, I'm happy not to have to go up against Hagun Seikun ourselves," Lionel said quietly as he stroked his chin.

Lionel, Gallardworth's most highly skilled lancer, had earned the title of Rhongomiant, and yet, it seemed even he didn't want to fight Xiaohui Wu directly.

Ernest himself couldn't deny that Xiaohui's sheer power and abilities were, in a word, outstanding.

Even with the unique strengths of his Orga Lux, the Lei-Glems, Ernest couldn't help but wonder whether even he would be able to defeat him himself.

"Unfortunately, they probably won't be able to field a full team, not in that state. That girl, in particular—Kirin Toudou, right?—she didn't look good. If I were her, I'd be more worried about making a full recovery." Kevin, leaning back on the sofa with his hands behind his head, seemed to be legitimately concerned for her well-being. As long as he wasn't on the battlefield, he would always take the side of a lady.

"…Given her state, I doubt she will be able to take part in the final," answered Percival, her face unreadable.

While the three other members were all sitting on the sofa, she alone stood leaning against the wall in near silence.

"Hmm… You're probably right about that." Ernest nodded.

"It does seem to be a little different, but I suspect she has a similar eye for detail as I do. She seems to have overdone it, however, so she probably won't be able to use it again for a while. Not to mention her other serious injuries."

Percival had an unusually keen sense of observation, one that allowed her to see through the true natures of those whom she encountered—and one that made it all but impossible to sneak a lie past her.

In Ernest's view, it was because of those eyes that homed in on the truth, and the unending sense of guilt that that entailed, that she had been chosen to wield the Holy Grail. The Holy Grail was even more selective than his own Orga Lux, and like the Runesword, it couldn't be deceived.

"Which means that it will be four against five, I suppose. There's no denying our advantage. They'll all be exhausted from their last match, while we've basically reached the final by default. Not to mention, our better training."

"...Hold on a minute, Lionel," Laetitia responded. "As true as that might be, you'd still better not let your guard down."

"I'm simply stating an objective fact." Lionel frowned, more in disappointment than anything else. "I don't mean to make light of them, nor to go easy on them, either."

Lionel always tried to evaluate things fairly. That often put him at odds with Kevin and also led to him quarreling with Laetitia, who tended to express herself more directly.

"Right, none of us here would treat an opponent that way, Letty." Kevin spoke lightly, as if in jest, but his eyes were serious.

They never treated their opponents with disdain, never cowered in the face of illusions, always fighting at their full strength to open up the path to victory—that was how Team Lancelot did things. Justice and order, truth and honesty—those were the symbols of Saint Gallardworth Academy.

And yet—

"I'm aware of that. I *am* a part of this team, you know. It's just..."

Turning away from Laetitia for a moment, Ernest glanced back at the air-window, once again showing Ayato in the middle of the stage.

Ayato Amagiri... He truly is magnificent. I look forward to—

But he stopped himself there, shaking his head with a bitter smile.

Don't. Don't finish that thought.

He rose to his feet, letting out a brief sigh as he tried to stifle the pain building in his chest. "Now then... I'm stepping out for little while. I'll leave everything to you."

"Huh? H-hold on a minute, Ernest!" Laetitia called out after him. "What do you mean you're stepping out? We need to plan for the match!"

Ernest, however, simply gave her a gentle smile before wordlessly leaving the room.

*

In Le Wolfe Black Institute's student council room...

"Tch! So Seidoukan pulled through...!" Dirk Eberwein practically spat the words out as he sat at his desk. He slammed his hand down on the button to shut the air-window from which he had been watching the match.

Neither Le Wolfe nor Dirk himself had been paying much attention to this year's Gryps. They had hired a mercenary team to fight on behalf of the school, but that was more of a face-saving measure than anything else, and it had more or less served its purpose by the time it had made its first entry.

As for whether Jie Long or Seidoukan made it to the championship, or indeed who ended up winning that match, Dirk wasn't particularly interested.

What had him annoyed was that it was *Ayato*'s team that had won.

Ayato Amagiri—Haruka Amagiri's younger brother and the wielder of the Ser Veresta.

Dirk had only met him in person once (although, strictly speaking, they had also seen each other at ceremonies and the like), but that was enough to know that he would be a problem. For Dirk, who viewed others as little more than chess pieces, Ayato was the worst kind of trouble imaginable. He was easily manipulated most of the time, but he would always manage to flip the board over at the most inopportune moment.

"I'd like to eliminate him entirely, and yet... Huh?"

His mobile had begun to ring. He set it to voice-only mode before opening a blank air-window.

"...*The demon and the false god are moving*," a gloomy voice reported.

"Hmm, just as I'd thought." Dirk frowned. Given the situation, this wasn't an unexpected development.

"*What do you want me to do?*"

"Keep monitoring them. But keep your distance. They'll know if you get too close."

"*Understood.*"

With that, the air-window snapped shut.

The operative wasn't one of Le Wolfe's Cats, but rather was one of Dirk's own agents. If he involved Grimalkin, the information would inevitably leak to the school's IEF, Solnage. He had to be selective with who he assigned to each task.

All the more so when the task in question involved the Golden Bough Alliance.

"What the hell are you thinking, Madiath Mesa...? If you're gonna try something, I'm not just gonna sit here idly," he muttered before opening five small air-windows.

He glared at the faces of each of the members of Saint Gallard-worth Academy's Team Lancelot in turn. There was a surprisingly detailed amount of information on each of them.

He had had the Gold Eyes do some reconnaissance a few days earlier. There was nothing unusual about gathering information on one's potential opponents during the Festa, and so it wouldn't have drawn attention to use Grimalkin for such a task. Not that he intended to use that information in the way that anyone could have been expecting.

He had already looked it all over several times now, and there wasn't much new there. Given the amount of detail they had already gathered, there probably wasn't much else left to dig up. Nor was there likely to be anything particularly useful that he could use to his advantage.

That was, leaving one of them aside.

Dirk closed the remaining air-windows one by one.

Ernest Fairclough, Laetitia Blanchard, Lionel Karsch, Kevin Holst…until finally only one remained open in front of him.

"Percival Gardner…"

Dirk had only ever been interested in this one—the user of the Holy Grail and Team Lancelot's newest member. Given that she was a newcomer, he had hoped there would be something to dig up on her, and yet…

Looking over her personal history, he couldn't contain his surprise.

It went far beyond what even he had expected.

As he stared at the face in that air-window, a stream of unpleasant memories seemed to spring back to life. His finger almost tried to close the air-window through sheer reflex, but he stayed his hand, clicking his tongue in distaste.

"I don't like it…but this *will* improve my hand."

He already held the joker, Orphelia Landlufen, but that alone wouldn't be enough to win.

If you were going to play against Madiath Mesa, you needed every advantage you could get.

Just then—

"Mr. President, would you like some coffee?" asked a dim-witted face in a newly opened air-window.

"Argh…" He found himself so put out that he couldn't even bring himself to shout back at her, merely opening the door to his office with an annoyed look. "Get in here."

"Hee-hee, Priscilla made some cookies. They look delicious, don't you think?"

"Ah…" Dirk put his head in his hands, trying to find a simple way to word his instructions. "Hey, Korona. I've got a job for you."

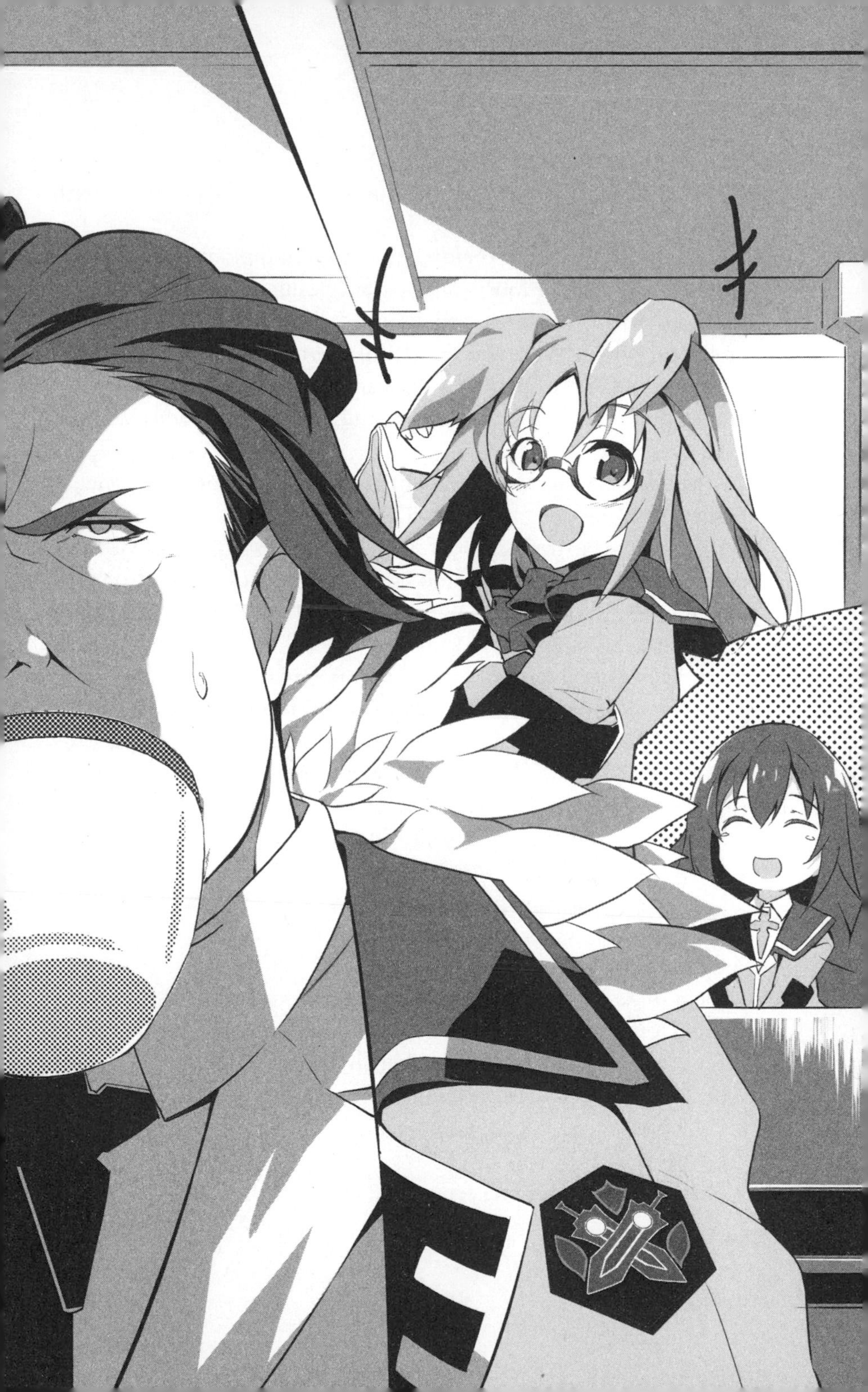

"Huh?"

"Come with me to the Gryps final tomorrow."

"Huh?! Really?!" she exclaimed, clapping her hands together with glee.

It went without saying that tickets to the championship match of a Festa were by far the most sought-after. Being his private secretary, she was, of course, permitted to join him in his private booth... or so one would have expected. While he didn't have much choice when it came to the opening and closing ceremonies, he hardly ever attended the matches themselves, and so this would be her first time attending.

"Yes! Thank you, Mr. President! I've always wanted to watch a Festa firsthand!" she squealed with delight.

Dirk let out a tired sigh before continuing softly: "Deliver this, before it starts. That's the job." He pulled a card out from his desk drawer, scribbling something on the front before flinging it toward her.

"Huh? Deliver it to who?"

"Do I have to answer that? Gallardworth's Team Lancelot."

"Oh...?" Korona tilted her head to one side, her expression puzzled. "I understand... I'm just a little surprised. Do you know them, Mr. President?"

"Shut up. That's none of your business." Dirk glared back at her.

Korona recoiled at the words.

"I'm only gonna say this once, so listen up. Don't go there in that stupid uniform. And don't give it to them directly. Just leave it at their office."

Each of Asterisk's six schools maintained a special office at the Sirius Dome during the course of the Festa, whose job it was to receive presents and fan mail on behalf of their contestants.

"B-but in that case, won't it take a while to reach them...?"

"That's not your concern. Don't worry about it. Just tell them it's from the institute."

"The institute?" Korona repeated. She clearly had no idea what he was talking about, but there was, of course, no need for her to know in the first place.

Dirk waved his hand to signal the end of their conversation, driving her out of the room.

"...Damn it, who would have thought it would come to this?" he muttered with an angry click of his tongue.

CHAPTER 5
LAMINA MORTIS

"Hmm... Well, she should be good to leave in around three days' time, I'd say," Director Jan Korbel told them in a nasal voice from Kirin's bedside. "The Ban'yuu Tenra's assessment is largely correct. Essentially, she's exhausted her prana. Although it *is* rare for someone who isn't a Strega or a Dante to burn up so much."

"And her eyes?" Ayato asked.

"Well, our tests didn't bring anything up, but it will be hard to tell until she awakens," the director answered as he stroked his mustache.

"I see..."

"In any event, what she needs is rest," he finished, departing with a casual wave. "I'll check in again later."

Claudia, from her seat in the corner of the room, let out a tired sigh. "Hmm... In other words, I suppose we don't need to worry about her injuries. I'm glad to hear that, and yet...without her, we're not going to have an easy time with tomorrow's match. I trust you all understand just how much of a challenge this is going to be?"

"..."

Ayato, Julis, and Saya all dropped their gazes without responding.

A heavy atmosphere lay over the four. To an outside observer, they no doubt looked as far from a championship team as could be imagined.

In a team battle, the loss of a member didn't just mean the loss of one person's fighting potential. Without Kirin, they wouldn't be able to use a good number of their coordination patterns, and they would also take a significant hit in both their offensive and defensive capabilities.

"And we're up against Gallardworth's Lancelot… Even at our full strength, I can't say whether we would win."

"…That doesn't mean we should give up without even trying." Saya clenched her fists resolutely. "Not when Kirin fought so hard for us to get here."

She herself had just woken up and had also undergone an examination, but fortunately, she had merely lost consciousness and would be fine to participate in the upcoming match. The other three had injuries of their own—but nothing so serious that they would have to pull out.

"Right. And I'm not going to give up on my dream. I'll be there even if I have to fight all by myself," Julis declared, her eyes gleaming.

"…A team can't compete without at least three members," Claudia reminded her.

"I know that! I'm just pointing out my resolve! Anyway… It's not like anyone else here is going to give up, now, is it?"

Claudia's shoulders shook with mirth. "It *is* true that I'm at a loss, though. No matter how I try to approach it, I simply can't think up a winning strategy… But I suppose we don't have much choice." She stood up from her chair and turned toward Ayato.

Julis and Saya both followed suit.

He nodded in understanding. "I feel the same way. No matter how strong they are, we have to win. For the team and for ourselves," he declared firmly. "If we're all in agreement on that, I guess we should go back to our dorms and get some rest. Tomorrow's match is at noon, after all. We probably won't be able to recover all our prana, but still…"

Since yesterday's troubles with the Night Emit, they had jumped from one battle to the next. Out of the four of them, Julis was in the worst shape. Being a Strega, her abilities consumed a lot of prana; and on top of that, her Rect Lux had been damaged in the last match, with only three of its remote units still in a usable state. There were spares, of course, but Rect Luxes required even more adjustment than regular ones, and there was little chance that she would be able to properly ready them in time for the match.

Under any other circumstances, Saya, too, would no doubt have liked to spend the night adjusting her own Luxes, but this time, she would have no choice but to leave everything to the Society for the Study of Meteoric Engineering. She didn't like giving her Luxes to others, but when asked, she had replied simply: "There's someone I trust there."

"In that case, let's call a car. Please wait a moment," Claudia said, pulling out her mobile device, when Ayato raised his hand.

"Um, sorry. I'll head back by myself. There's someone I want to see first."

"What? At this hour?" Julis asked dubiously.

Saya, however, tugged at her sleeve. "Julis, this is *the* hospital."

"—! Right, your sister…" She glanced down at her feet in embarrassment.

"Well, I just wanted to drop in."

"Say hi for me, too, Ayato… I'd like to see her as well, though…" Saya pouted.

That was understandable. She had known Haruka since she was a child, after all.

In fact, Ayato had asked Director Korbel about letting her visit several times, but the special treatment area was accessible only by authorized individuals, and it seemed that Saya, not being a direct family member, hadn't been given permission to enter.

"I could tag along with you. And besides, it isn't like we aren't close enough. I'm like family, aren't I?" Saya said sullenly.

"…I don't think that will work," Julis interrupted coolly.

"*I* would like to meet Ayato's sister one day, too," Claudia added with an amused smile. "I'm sure she's a wonderful person."

"...In that case, you should be able to see her pretty soon, right?" Julis, her arms crossed, said with a chuckle.

"Huh?" Ayato had no idea what she meant.

"Your wish is to wake her up, right? So all we have to do is win one more match. Then we'll all be able to see her... Right?"

Julis looked somewhat embarrassed, but her words touched Ayato's heart. "Right. Yes, exactly."

Just one more match.

All they had to do was win, and he'd be able to talk to her again.

"You can be pretty sharp every now and then, Julis," Saya commented.

"Indeed, I'm moved," Claudia added.

"...What do you mean, *every now and then*?"

As he watched Julis and Saya glare at each other across the room, Ayato couldn't help but let out a light laugh. "Well then, see you all tomorrow."

"Ah, Ayato. Let me know when you want to come back. I'll arrange a car to pick you up."

"Thanks, Claudia," Ayato responded, touched by her concern.

With nothing else to discuss, he gently stroked Kirin's head one last time before leaving the room.

*

"Hmm, hmm, hmm..."

Sylvia hummed to herself as she strolled through the corridor on the top floor of Queenvale Academy for Young Ladies' Twin Hall.

She was happier than she had found herself in a long time.

That wasn't just because Ayato's Team Enfield had made it through to the championship, nor simply because all his efforts thus far had paid off. No, those things were, of course, wonderful; but even more than that, she was overjoyed by the fact that they were now viewed not as toys, but dangers, to the IEFs.

In Asterisk, the integrated enterprise foundations were practically the world, and it was all but impossible to oppose them. She couldn't be more grateful to Ayato and the others for proving that, no matter how calculating they were, no matter how much they thought they could treat their students as mere tools, that it was indeed possible to strike back.

She was thrilled beyond words.

"...And you were pretty cool, too, Ayato."

Their semifinal match had been a fierce one, and Ayato had been on the back foot against Hagun Seikun from the very beginning—but then love, as they say, is blind to one's imperfections.

She was, of course, worried about Kirin Toudou's injuries, but according to the official announcement released just a short while ago, her life wasn't in danger, though it was unlikely she would be able to compete in the championship.

It would be difficult to win against Team Lancelot fighting one member short, but given how Ayato and the others had overcome every obstacle thus far, Sylvia remained hopeful.

I'll have to go cheer them on! she thought as she reached the office of Queenvale's executive chairwoman, Petra Kivilehto, knocking quietly on the door as she tried to make her face appear normal.

"Petra, can I come in?"

The door opened without a sound. As she entered the room—

"I suppose congratulations are in order," Petra called out.

"...What are you talking about?"

The older woman's voice was as cool and composed as ever, rendering her emotions all but unreadable. She was standing in front of a wide window overlooking the brightly lit nighttime cityscape, staring at Sylvia through the visor covering her eyes. "Your friend, Ayato Amagiri, and his team made it through to the championship, after all," she continued.

"Oh, that," she replied, her composure slipping. She put her hands on her hips, trying to keep her elation from showing too much. "Yes, they did. But you didn't call me here just to say that, did you?"

At this, Petra merely opened an air-window in total silence, casting it toward her.

"And this is?"

The air-window showed the faces of several Queenvale students.

"They're members of Benetnasch... Or perhaps it would be more accurate to say that they *were* members of Benetnasch."

Claudia's expression suddenly stiffened. "What do you mean?"

"I decided to do some digging of my own into that organization—the Golden Bough Alliance. I was having them look into it."

"...Why is this the first I've heard about it?"

The Golden Bough Alliance: a mysterious organization that seemed to have something to do with her former teacher, Ursula Svend. There was no direct evidence proving its existence, but according to Petra, the name had been picked up by Queenvale's intelligence networks after Sylvia had intensified her search for her missing friend—or more specifically, after she had begun looking into Orga Luxes.

That being the case, the two couldn't be unrelated.

Even so, Sylvia had been unable to locate either Ursula or anyone else related to the organization. And a name alone wasn't enough to do anything.

But it looked like Petra had done some digging of her own.

"You do know that I'm under no obligation to report this to you, don't you?"

Sylvia almost flared up at Petra's curt manner of speaking, but she forced herself to keep her cool. Under any other circumstances, she would have been able to brush such comments aside without worry, but things were different when it came to Ursula.

Petra ought to have understood that, which meant she was intentionally trying to provoke her.

"...Hmm. It looks like you're calm enough to talk about this sensibly," Petra remarked.

"Will you stop trying to test me?"

Sylvia couldn't bring herself to be angry. She, too, was under no obligation to report to her, and had yet to tell her about her encounter with Ursula—or at least, the person who had once been Ursula—at the Gran Colosseo. She wasn't exactly sure why she was so reluctant to involve the woman, but it no doubt had something to do with that mysterious Orga Lux. So in a way, they were both keeping secrets from each other.

That said, since Petra was monitoring Sylvia's actions, at least to some extent, it was possible she already knew something. In that respect, Petra undeniably had an advantage.

"This is a dangerous matter, Sylvie. I still haven't been able to find the whereabouts of those girls."

"And you gave such a dangerous job to Benetnasch?"

Queenvale's intelligence organization specialized in the control and manipulation of information and wasn't as proficient as those of the other schools when it came to combat or subterfuge. When something called for a genuinely dangerous investigation, it was better to call in their integrated enterprise foundation's own forces—as Galaxy had done just the other day.

"For now, I've merely been looking into things myself. If I wanted to involve anyone higher than Benetnasch, I would need the authorization of the board of directors. But I'll admit now that I underestimated this Alliance..." Despite her words, Petra's tone remained cool and detached. "I *have* been able to learn one thing, however. It seems that someone called Lamina Mortis, the Blade of Death, is involved with this Golden Bough Alliance in some capacity."

"...Lamina Mortis?"

"He used to be a regular contestant in the Eclipse."

"—!" Sylvia's eyes opened wide in surprise before narrowing in suspicion. "What's this? You're willing to tell me about the Eclipse now?"

Sylvia and Petra—or technically, the integrated enterprise foundation W&W—had a contractual relationship. Sylvia's goal was, it went without saying, to locate Ursula, and while W&W would monitor any actions that she undertook to that end, they would neither interfere nor cooperate. In exchange, she worked for Queenvale as a songstress, both promoting the school and producing considerable income for it.

Sylvia had long since surmised that the IEFs knew much more about the Eclipse than they let on, but there was no way that Petra would have divulged that to her. At least, that had been the way of things until now.

"I decided that it would be in your best interests to know this. So that you understand just how dangerous what you're doing really is."

"..." Sylvia had her doubts whether that was the real reason but resolved to listen on in silence.

"You may have misunderstood this, but what W&W knows about the Eclipse is only a small part of the equation. Danilo Bertoni was the one who organized it, and he did it in a way that, in principle, there would be no direct relationship leading back to the foundations. Because no matter how you look at it, that event was clearly overkill. It would reflect poorly on anyone who got tied up in it."

"In principle...? So there *was* some kind of connection?"

"It appears that some people went there as spectators."

Sylvia wasn't particularly surprised by this revelation.

"To the extent that the foundations were willing to tolerate its existence, there *was* some utility value to the Eclipse," Petra continued. "It had a number of passionate enthusiasts, you see. Anyway, after Danilo died, and the Eclipse was exposed by the city guard, the foundations had the investigation shut down to keep those connections from getting out. Danilo worked for Solnage, after all, and they didn't want to be tarnished by his actions. But more than that, there seems to have been some secret that all the foundations, to one extent or another, wanted to keep from getting out..."

"That's enough." Sylvia didn't want to hear any more. She already felt slightly tainted. "What does that have to do with this Lamina Mortis?"

"I'm afraid that not even we know the details. In principle, like in the Festa, contestants in the Eclipse had to be students at one of the schools, but there seem to have been cases where they would compete against other fighters selected by the organizers. Lamina Mortis seems to have been one of those."

"...Was he strong?"

"As strong as his name suggests."

Lamina Mortis—it was enough to make her hair stand on end.

Sylvia had tried to look into the Eclipse herself, but all she had learned was that patronage was restricted to a select number of highly discerning individuals, while participation was limited only to those of a corresponding level of prowess.

"A battle against Lamina Mortis was more execution than anything else. It seems that his cruelty and savagery made him particularly popular among the Eclipse's sponsors. Although, he didn't make an appearance particularly often."

Sylvia couldn't bring herself to respond. It sounded like the lowest kind of event imaginable.

"As I said, participation wasn't limited to students. This Lamina Mortis seems to have been a somewhat older man. He always covered his face with a mask, so no one seems to know his true identity. Based on his skill, however, he must be a well-known fighter of some sort."

"...A mask?" Sylvia repeated dubiously.

Maybe things had been different in the distant past, but in this day and age, Sylvia couldn't help but wonder whether it was really possible to hide one's identity that way. She herself often went out in disguise and understood that the key to remaining hidden was to not draw attention to oneself, to hide one's presence and blend into the crowd. With a little bit of effort, that wasn't particularly difficult.

That assumed, however, that one wasn't already the focus of people's attention. If the Eclipse's patrons were as discerning as Petra said, any attempt at disguise would no doubt merely foster further intrigue. And if this Lamina Mortis was indeed famous, then a mask wouldn't be able to hide his build or height nor, for that matter, his individual fighting style.

"Anyway, this is my second piece of advice. The darkness that you're trying to penetrate goes much deeper than you think." For once, there was an unusual tinge of emotion in her voice.

As per the terms of their contract, Petra was unable to try to stop Sylvia. She understood that well enough. Nor would she be able to persuade her into giving up on her search. But she could, perhaps, help her to understand just what she was getting into.

If what she said was true, both that mysterious Orga Lux and this Lamina Mortis were involved in what had happened to Ursula in some way.

The Golden Bough Alliance…

Sylvia glanced to the side, casting her gaze through the window to the cityscape below as a cold chill ran up her spine.

*

"…Hagun Seikun was strong. I don't think I've fought anyone that strong since my last practice duel with you. Still, Kirin beat him. She really is amazing." Ayato was trying to keep his mind occupied by relating all manner of things to his comatose sister.

He told her about the day's events, fond memories he had with her, his friends—practically anything that came to mind. But even he was aware that, at times like this, he must have come across as incredibly childish.

Of course, Haruka, lying in her hospital bed, didn't respond to any of it.

"And then everyone kept saying how much they want to meet you. Saya, in particular, was disappointed at not being able to come here yet. But if she could come, I'm sure it would be you who would be the surprised one. She really hasn't changed at all since then…"

He stopped there, unable to go on.

A strange melancholy fell over him every time he came here to see her. It was an indescribable feeling, a sense of relief and fondness, mixed in with an inescapable touch of unease.

Haruka hadn't changed at all from how he remembered her, from how she had been the last time they had spoken.

But that was six years ago, and of course, Ayato had grown considerably since then.

He was now practically an adult. He had changed, but she remained the same. He couldn't help but feel as if they had become irreparably estranged.

If she were to wake up and see him as he was today, what kind of face would she make, what would she say?

"...I'd better get going, Haru," he said, getting up from his chair.

Even so, that didn't change the fact that the wish most dear to him was to find a way to awaken her.

Which was why he had no choice but to win tomorrow's match.

"Hmm...?" He glanced around as he stepped out of his sister's hospital room. He'd thought he had heard something, but there was no one in sight.

He was in a special, underground section of the hospital, accessible only by a very select few individuals. He had come there countless times before, but the only time he had ever seen anyone else down there was when he had first been shown around.

And yet...

"—!"

He suddenly noticed a presence in the shadows of the corridor far ahead of him, and all but reflexively, he adopted a defensive posture.

The figure, dressed in a hooded robe, clearly wasn't one of the hospital staff. On top of that, Ayato had met this person before.

"You...!"

It was the same woman who had attacked Sylvia during the Gran Colosseo, her former teacher, Ursula Svend—or at least, the body of Ursula Svend.

"Stop," the hooded figure said impassively as Ayato reached for the Ser Veresta. "I have no quarrel with you."

"...Then what do you want?"

Ayato could hardly accept that her presence here was a coincidence.

"Follow me. There's someone who wants to see you," she said before heading off down the corridor.

After a brief moment of hesitation, Ayato made up his mind.

He knew he should contact Sylvia, but he himself still didn't understand the situation. There would no doubt be unforeseen consequences if either acted rashly.

So he resolved to follow after the hooded figure alone.

It might have been the middle of the night, but even so, there was something unnatural about the fact that there was no one else around. Perhaps the woman simply knew the hospital so well as to avoid bumping into anyone else, but something seemed inexplicably off.

"...Here," she said, coming to a stop outside a large courtyard.

The space was almost the size of a small park. Amid the lush, well-tended trees stood a lone, masked man.

"Welcome, Ayato Amagiri."

There was something familiar about his voice, his figure, though Ayato couldn't pinpoint exactly what.

He was sure he knew that man, and yet, for some reason, the name wouldn't come to mind, as if a haze lay heavy over his thoughts.

"Ah, you needn't bother trying to see through the mask. This place is under my friend's control. You won't be able to recognize me here."

Ayato found it hard to believe the man's words, and yet, he had spoken so assuredly.

The woman had indeed demonstrated some kind of mind control the last time he had encountered her, but to think that it was strong enough to affect one's sense of recognition...

"Strictly speaking, I don't even need the mask. Think of it more as a matter of style... Well then, let me introduce myself. When I wear this mask, I go by the name of Lamina Mortis."

"Lamina Mortis..."

"And this is Varda, my associate," he added, placing a hand on her shoulder.

Varda, expressionless, immediately brushed that hand aside, glaring up at her companion.

"Hurry up and get it over with. I have other things to do."

"All right, all right, there's no need to be in such a hurry," Mortis said with a shrug and a smirk.

"...What do you want with me?" Ayato asked, tightening his grip on the Ser Veresta's activator so he could act at a moment's notice.

"Oh, it's nothing major. I wanted to give you a hand."

"Give me a hand?" Ayato furrowed his brow.

"As things stand, your team is in a bad place ahead of tomorrow's championship. You understand that, don't you?"

"—!" All of a sudden, Ayato released his energy, activating the Ser Veresta—but for some reason, its blade was quivering slightly, and it seemed to be giving off a faint noise. It almost seemed as it if was trying to warn him of something.

It's reacting to them...?

"Speaking for myself, I'm on your side here. I'd only be too happy to see you take the crown at this year's Gryps," the man continued. A Lux had appeared in his hands, too, from which a huge crimson blade slowly emerged.

No...

It was no regular Lux. Ayato had never seen it before in person, but staring at it now, he couldn't be surer.

It was an Orga Lux, and like his own Ser Veresta, one of the famed Four Colored Runeswords.

"...The Raksha-Nada!"

The Blade of Red Mist was supposed to have been sealed away. Ayato had no idea why it was in the possession of the man in front of him, but this was no time to worry about that.

The glowing weapon, like a sudden gale, came rushing toward him.

Taken aback by the sudden ferocity of the attack, Ayato hurried to defend himself with the Ser Veresta.

"*Ugh...!*"

The impact was heavy—and so powerful as to leave his arms numb. The paving stones at his feet began to crack as he braced to keep himself from being overcome.

"How is this supposed to be giving me a hand?!" Ayato shouted.

Their swords still locked, Lamina Mortis said nothing, merely flashing him a composed smile, until all of a sudden, he pulled away and lashed out from another direction.

Ayato managed to dodge the oncoming crimson blur, but Mortis quickly flowed into a second, then a third attack, forcing him to remain on the defensive.

Both the Raksha-Nada and the Ser Veresta were relatively large weapons, so there could be little denying that Lamina Mortis, with his superior physique, had the advantage.

On top of that, he was more skilled at a technical level, too.

Damn it... Why do they all have to come at once?!

Yesterday, it had been Bujinsai Yabuki, today, Xiaohui Wu, and now this guy—each far stronger than he was.

Moreover, his current opponent seemed to be no less formidable than Xiaohui Wu. Ayato was having a hard time even gauging the depths of his abilities.

"Why are you doing this?!" Ayato demanded over the clashing of their blades.

Lamina Mortis's lips curled in a faint smile. "I told you, didn't I? I'm giving you a hand," he answered calmly.

Ayato was sure he had heard that voice before, but to his frustration, his memories just wouldn't piece together.

"Then, stop this! I don't have any reason to fight you!" Ayato called out as he repelled the Raksha-Nada once more and took a few steps back.

His breathing ragged, he glanced at his surroundings. Fortunately, there didn't appear to be anyone else around. In that case, escape was always an option.

Given the match tomorrow, he couldn't afford to waste any more energy.

"Hmm, no reason, you say...? Very well. Then how about this?" Lamina Mortis said softly as he lowered the Raksha-Nada. "It was I who cut down your sister."

"—!" At that moment, Ayato's vision turned bloodred. "What did you just say?" His body trembled as an uncontrollable ferocity began to well up from deep inside him.

"I was a regular contestant in the Eclipse. Then, six years ago, I faced your sister in the arena... I'm sure you know the rest."

Ayato didn't even wait for him to finish before launching himself toward the man.

He shortened the distance between them in the blink of an eye, slashing downward from above.

"What do we have here...?" There was a touch of admiration in Lamina Mortis's voice as he parried the attack.

"Keep talking! Tell me what happened...!"

"Heh-heh, impressive! So you know enough to keep your anger in check, letting it fuel but not overcome you. Haru trained you well."

The man's baiting, however, only managed to inflame Ayato's rage further, leading him to lash out with a flurry of thrusts and slashes.

"But now that it's come to this...," Mortis murmured under his breath as he effortlessly parried each and every attack. "I suppose I have no choice..."

Ayato ground his teeth together in rage as he made the Ser Veresta move faster still—yet, the blade didn't even come close to grazing his opponent.

"Argh!"

"What's stopping you? Strike me down. If you defeat me, you'll finally be able to learn everything you want to know, won't you?" Mortis called out, holding the Raksha-Nada in one hand.

His voice sounded almost as if he were trying to test him.

But no, this isn't a test...

Ayato drove the thought from his mind. He had to keep his focus on what was in front of him. If he divided his attention, that would be the end for him.

He had already released his full energy once today. He still had a little left in him, but he wouldn't be able to drag it out.

In that case...

He knew it was a reckless move, but he stepped forward anyway.

"Amagiri Shinmei Style, Middle Technique—*Nine-Fanged Blade!*"

A ninefold sequence of five thrusts and four slashing strikes.

"Oh?" Lamina Mortis, however, parried each of the attacks single-handed.

Not only that, but no sooner had Ayato completed the technique

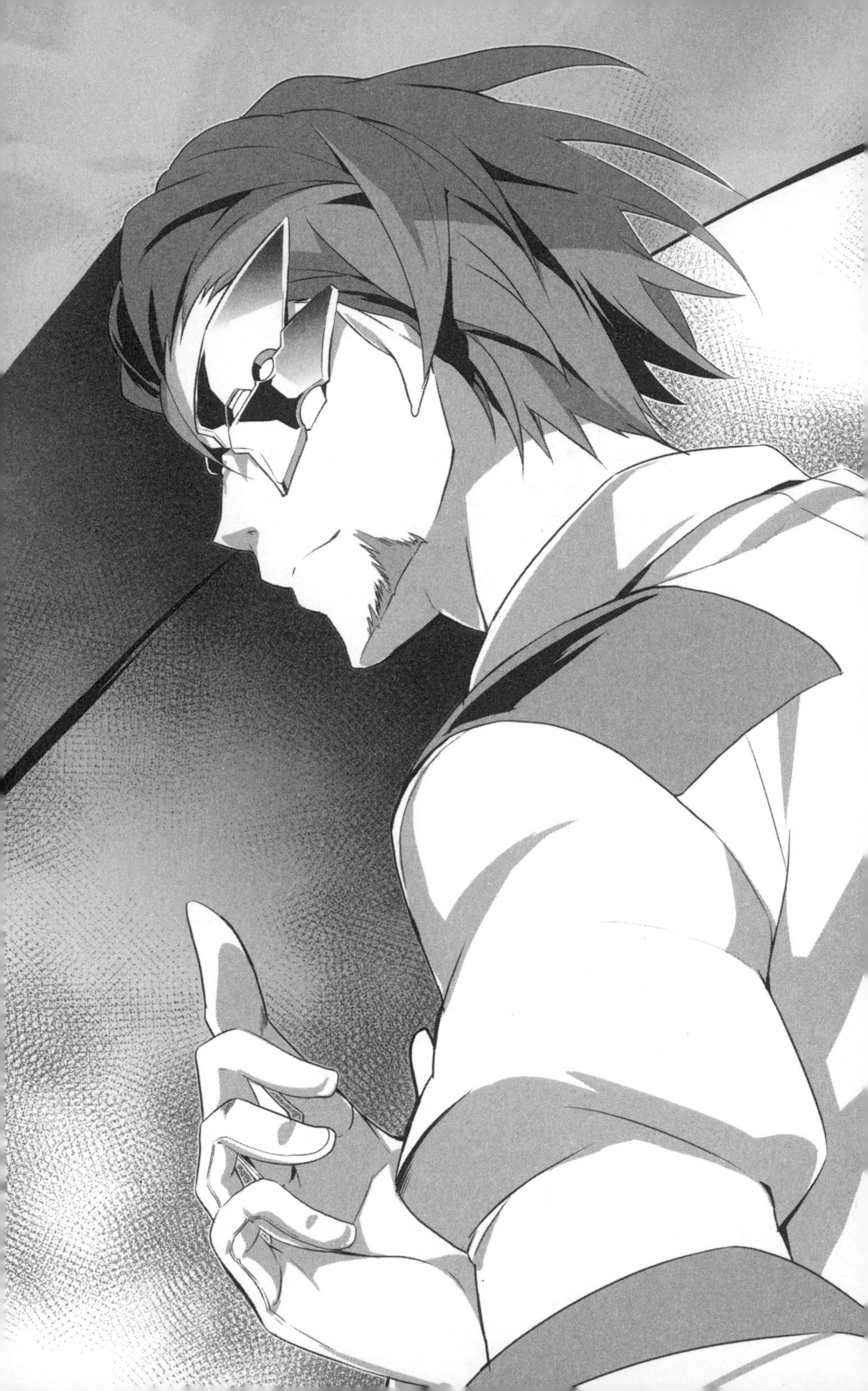

than his opponent drove a powerful kick into his abdomen, sending him crashing across the paving stones.

"*Ughn...!*"

He picked himself up immediately, but his breathing was ragged, his heart racing.

His opponent was too strong. Exhausted from consecutive battles, Ayato was on the verge of being overpowered.

Even so, I can't let this chance go!

He mustered his remaining strength, bracing himself with the Ser Veresta, when he noticed that the blade was once again trembling and emitting that faint noise.

"Huh...?"

"What...?"

Lamina Mortis muttered as well, glancing at his own blade.

And that was when—

"Now, what do we have here?"

—Ayato followed the relaxed voice that had come from the edge of the courtyard to see a young man armed with a burning-white Orga Lux strolling toward them.

CHAPTER 6
LIFTING THE CURTAIN

"Ernest Fairclough..." Ayato stared in surprise at the figure of the approaching young man.

Ernest, the Lei-Glems clasped tightly in his hand, came to a stop beside him with a charismatic smile.

"What a coincidence, Amagiri. I didn't think I'd find you in a place like this. Now then," he began, his expression turning serious as he cast his gaze toward Mortis. "What's going on here?"

His voice was much colder than Ayato was used to hearing, and Ayato found himself swallowing his breath at the intimidating aura radiating from him.

So this is what Pendragon is like when he's serious... He's a completely different person than at the Gran Colosseo.

Lamina Mortis, however, completely unperturbed, merely called out to Varda: "I thought I asked you to clear this place out?"

"...Don't be unreasonable," she answered in an almost-mechanical voice. "You know that mind control and isolation boundaries aren't fully compatible with each other. It might be possible to maintain both against an average person, but not against someone like this."

"Oh dear, are you ignoring me? But maybe trying to dissuade someone who would ambush a contestant the day before an important match was doomed from the start?" Ernest lowered the tip of the Lei-Glems toward Lamina Mortis.

"Be careful. He's stronger than he lets on," Ayato whispered as he readied the Ser Veresta.

"I guessed as much from your exchange... Is that the Raksha-Nada?"

Ernest, it seemed, was sharp-eyed.

On closer inspection, the crimson blade was letting out a faint buzzing sound much like those of the Lei-Glems and Ser Veresta.

"This is an important occasion. It may well be the first time in all of Asterisk's history that we've had three of the Four Colored Runeswords gathered in one place. I would very much love to savor this moment...but I'm afraid it's time." With that, Lamina Mortis returned the Raksha-Nada to its holder before leaping backward into the distance. "I can't say it went according to plan, but I've achieved my purpose here," he called out. "I look forward to tomorrow's match!"

"Wait!" Ayato shouted as he attempted to leap after the departing figure, when Varda appeared in his path.

"You'll remain here," she said, the piece of manadite—no, urm-manadite—inlaid in the necklace at her breast letting out a deep, jet-black light.

So Sylvia was right...

It looked like she had hit the mark in surmising that it was an Orga Lux that had usurped Ursula's body. Its ability was no doubt mind control, and the cost of using it was the loss of one's own body.

"Ernest! Watch out for that black light!" Ayato, having already faced her once, called out in warning.

He readied himself to counterattack with the Ser Veresta, but the black light soon began to wrap around its urm-manadite core. He couldn't tell what would happen if he followed through with it.

However—

"No need to worry!" Ernest answered, as with a brilliant flash, the Lei-Glems cut straight through the black light.

"—!" That's..."

While they differed in their specific abilities, each of the Four Colored Runeswords was essentially impossible to defend against. That being the case, it shouldn't have come as a surprise that he had been able to dispel her ability.

"These Runeswords, breaking through my abilities whenever they please...," Varda murmured darkly as she gathered yet more black light into both hands, the writhing shadow quickly taking the form of a huge ax.

At that moment, Ayato attempted to leap past her in pursuit of Lamina Mortis.

Once again, however, she blocked his advance before rushing toward him with her ax of black lightning. Ayato tried to fend her off, but the force of the impact went far beyond what he had been expecting.

"Ugh..."

"Amagiri!" Ernest tried to fight his way through to him, but Varda blocked him.

Ernest successfully evaded her counterattack, but as he did so, his face turned pale with shock. "This... This is no ordinary lady..."

Ayato had assumed that mind control was her only ability, but that had been a mistake. They could forget about taking her on individually—she was skilled enough to hold them both back simultaneously.

"Unlike my previous body, this one knows how to hold its own in a fight. Don't take it lightly."

Of course. Ursula Svend had taught Queenvale's number-one fighter and the runner-up from the last Lindvolus. He should have expected that she would be a formidable opponent.

And yet—

"You are indeed strong. Frankly speaking, I'm impressed...," Ernest said. "And yet, I doubt you can win against us both."

Right. There was no doubting Varda's skill, but she wasn't at the level of Lamina Mortis. Ayato had only faced him the once, but that was clear enough.

"Indeed. I could take either of you alone, but not together," Varda admitted without hesitation. "But that doesn't concern me. He should be long gone by now. In which case... There's no need for me to keep this area sealed off."

No sooner had she finished speaking than the strange, oppressive feeling that enveloped them lifted.

Ernest seemed to have noticed it as well. "That's...," he began as he glanced around in suspicion.

At that moment, Varda released a burst of black light more intense than any Ayato had seen before.

A ferocious pain tore through his skull, sending him crashing to his knees.

So that's how much power she was putting into her boundary...!

The fact that she had turned it all against him now meant she was serious this time.

"Argh..."

Ernest carved the Lei-Glems through the cloud of black light, but for what seemed like the longest time, it refused to abate.

When finally the pain stopped, Varda was nowhere to be seen.

*

"...Dear me. Are you all right?" Ernest asked as he held out his hand.

"I think so," Ayato answered as he was helped to his feet.

"I've contacted the city guard, so they shouldn't be too long now. You can tell me what that was about once they arrive."

"Sorry to get you caught up in all this," Ayato answered, his head bowed. "But thanks. If not for your help..."

To be honest, he had no idea what might have happened if Ernest hadn't shown up.

Ernest, however, gave him a brilliant, almost-sparkling smile as he shook his head. "Not at all. I'm just glad you weren't hurt. I'm looking forward to facing you myself tomorrow, after all."

"...Me too." Ayato grinned back.

But at the same time, he was filled with questions. True, with the exception of the damage he had taken during the semifinal, he was largely uninjured. The worst that he had received from Lamina Mortis was the kick that had thrown him to the ground.

Mortis was at least as powerful as Xiaohui Wu—and probably more so. It simply didn't make sense that Ayato had been able to face him and escape unharmed.

Unless he was trying not to injure me...? But in that case, why would he have gone to all this trouble...?

Ayato had no idea what the man had been hoping to achieve.

But he stopped himself there. There was no understanding something that couldn't be understood. Even thinking about it was pointless.

Instead, he directed his next question at Ernest: "By the way... What were you doing here?"

Ernest, of course, ought to have been preparing for tomorrow's match as well. Given Kirin's condition, Ayato had reason enough to visit the hospital, but Ernest's team had won their match by default, and so, they were perfectly able-bodied.

"I came to see my sister."

"Oh, Team Kaguya...," Ayato murmured, suddenly remembering the team from Queenvale that had been earmarked as this year's dark horse.

They had been soundly defeated in the quarterfinals, with several of their members sustaining major injuries. Ernest's sister, Sophia, must have been one of them.

"As her brother, I thought I should check in," he said, his expression suddenly unreadable. "But I wonder whether I still have the right to call myself that..."

"Huh?"

"I'm the reason she came to Asterisk," he said with a tired sigh. "It sounds like she wanted to win the Festa so she could take over the Fairclough name, setting me free to live as I pleased... Such a foolish girl..."

"Setting you free...?"

Ernest let out a resigned chuckle. "From the bonds of family. She was involved in an accident, a long time ago. She ended up hurting a good friend of mine. That led to a rift between my friend and me—no, between my friend's family and our own, I suppose. She still blames herself for that, it seems." Ernest spoke quietly, but he seemed to become somewhat more animated when he said the word *friend*, a hint of nostalgia entering his voice. "She—my friend—was very important to me, and there's no denying that the only time I could really feel at ease was when I was with her. So it isn't as if I can't understand Sophia's sense of guilt… But it's all in the past now." He stopped there, setting upright a bench that must have been knocked over during the previous fight, before urging Ayato to join him.

As Ayato sat down beside him, Ernest tilted his head back to stare up at the glimmering night sky. "I've come to accept the bonds of house and family. You could say that I've managed to tame that sense of confinement. I thought that Sophia had realized that, but I suppose it must have still looked like a burden to her."

Not once did Ernest look in his direction. He half sounded as if he were talking to himself. Even so, there was something Ayato wanted to ask. "Is it really such a burden?"

He didn't know much about the Fairclough house, nor about Ernest's particular circumstances.

And yet, the young man sitting across from him had always come across as somewhat *too* perfect. Ernest was the kind of person whose fame seemed to just keep on rising to new heights. Endowed with strength, kindness, nobility, and a broad-minded attitude—and with a tenure as student council president at Saint Gallardworth Academy that simply couldn't be faulted. And yet, Ayato had a hard time believing anyone could truly live up to such lofty standards.

"No one can live apart from their surroundings. So the question is how to take control of one's circumstances. I'm fortunate enough to have been blessed with the resources necessary to do that."

It was a vague response, but the words rang true. The way Ayato saw it, there could be no doubting that Ernest would be able to meet whatever bonds or expectations that were thrust upon him—no matter whether they were born out of kindness or ill will.

"Selflessness might be the guiding principle for all of us at Gallard-worth, and yet… You might not know this, because we're cautioned against putting our desires into words, but there are many among us who would like nothing more than to win at the Festa and have our selfish wishes come true."

"Huh?" Ayato stared at him blankly. He had no idea what Ernest wished for. "In that case, why are you…?"

"Some of us do it for a house or family, for example," Ernest continued.

Ayato, however, still didn't understand. "In that case…"

"You must have noticed how many of our students come from old families and supposedly noble pedigrees. It isn't at all common for Genestella to be accepted by such families. If you want to find somewhere you can belong among such people, you need to find a way to prove your worth. That is, by winning at the Festa and using your wish to benefit them in some way." Ernest's voice was startlingly cold as he spoke. "Laetitia, Kevin, Lionel, Doroteo, Elliot—the same goes for all of them. But there are exceptions, too, I suppose. In my team, Percival seems to have a wish of her own, for instance."

No one can live apart from their surroundings, Ayato repeated in silence. The words seemed to carry a strange weight.

"I've gone on a little, haven't I? Don't let what I said bother you," Ernest offered, flashing him a friendly smile.

Footsteps could be heard gathering in the distance—the city guard, no doubt.

"Well, we might as well get this over with." With that, Ernest rose to his feet, signaling the end of the conversation.

At that moment, Helga Lindwall appeared at the edge of the courtyard, leading a squad of Stjarnagarm officers.

Ayato, troubled in a way that he couldn't easily describe, rose to meet her.

*

The following morning, in the team's prep room at the Sirius Dome, Ayato recounted the night's events to his assembled team members.

"Wh-why are you always letting yourself get caught up in things like that?" Julis demanded angrily, but she soon trailed off. Her face turned scarlet as she mouthed something to herself in silence, then sunk limply into her chair.

"Ayato is always getting himself in trouble. You should be used to it by now, Julis," Saya said with a smug look.

Claudia, however, wasn't amused. "Even so, this is going a little *too* far. We can't overlook it this time."

"Oh? Since when are you prone to worrying, Claudia? But only when it comes to Ayato, it seems," Saya pointed out.

"Not at all," she answered with a smile.

It was clear, however, that her composure this time was entirely feigned.

"Claudia... You actually look pretty cute, for once."

"I don't know how I'm supposed to feel when you say that, Julis," she answered, her expression a delicate mix of happiness and chagrin. "Anyway," she began, clearing her throat and turning to Ayato, her countenance once again serious. "There are things I want to ask you about that, but we should save them for later. And there's something I have to tell you all, too."

"What do you mean?" Ayato asked, but Claudia quickly cut him off.

"Later. Right now, we need to think about the match." Letting out a resigned sigh, she opened several air-windows. "This is a simulation based on my calculations..."

"...That doesn't look good," Julis grunted in concern.

"It's practically a slaughterhouse," Saya added.

"Indeed. As you can see, starting off with a handicap severely limits our options. Which means that our best strategy will be..." She paused for a moment to close all but one of the air-windows.

"A full-frontal attack...," Ayato murmured.

"Exactly." Claudia nodded. "Team Lancelot specializes in team battles—to such an extent that they can practically function as a single, integrated unit. We won't be able to counter that through tricks or artifice, meaning that the only practical option available to us is to put everything into our offense. But if any one of us makes a mistake, we will no doubt be taken down immediately."

"But we're already at a disadvantage. If we take them head-on, how will we be able to break through?" Saya asked uneasily.

Ayato, however, shook his head. "That may be so, but it's what I was thinking of, too."

"Oh? That isn't like you." Julis sounded surprised, but she, too, had broken out into a broad grin.

"If our odds of winning aren't very high anyway, I, at least, want to fight in a way that I can look back on without regret... That goes for all of you, too, right?" he added, glancing around at the other three.

"...Yeah."

"No objections here."

"Then, it's decided."

At that moment, Ayato's mobile began to ring. As soon as he saw the name indicated on the display, he hurriedly opened an air-window.

"Kirin, are you okay?!"

"Y-yes, thanks to all of you..."

No sooner did her face appear before them than Julis, Saya, and Claudia all let out sighs of relief.

"So you're finally awake?"

"That's a relief."

"Indeed, that's all that matters."

The three each smiled at her warmly.

Ayato, of course, was of the same opinion.

She seemed to still be lying in bed, but thankfully, her complexion looked much better than the previous night.

"We were so worried... You wouldn't open your eyes... How are they, by the way?"

"Ah, yes, everything still looks a little bright, but it isn't serious. A-anyway... I'm really, truly sorry!" On the other side of the air-window, Kirin bowed so suddenly and so deeply that her head filled the display. *"You'll be short one team member, all because of me..."*

"What are you saying, Kirin? It's thanks to you that we were even able to make it this far," Ayato pointed out.

"Right. We're nothing but grateful to you," Julis said firmly.

"You were the only one of us who could defeat Hagun Seikun." Claudia nodded. "If anything, you should be puffing your chest out in pride!"

"We won't let your efforts go to waste," Saya added. "We're going to win this match. Just wait and see."

Kirin lifted a hand to wipe away the tears that had begun to brim in the corners of her eyes at this wave of encouragement. *"All right. I might not be able to do much from here, but I'll be supporting you all the way!"* The areas around her eyes had turned red, but she shone with a brave, hopeful smile.

Ayato and the others exchanged wordless glances before nodding confidently back at her.

∗

Meanwhile, at the Sirius Dome…

"Everyone! How are our preparations?" Ernest asked of Team Lancelot's assembled team members in their own prep room.

"I'm ready to go at any moment now." Laetitia nodded.

"As good as ever. No problems here," Lionel added.

"Well, yesterday I ended up turning down invitations from so many beautiful ladies, just so I could get some rest," Kevin answered. "But I guess we've all got to do our part."

All three were brimming with confidence, each, it seemed, already assured of victory.

It wasn't arrogance or conceit that led them to think that way, but rather their excessive pride at their own abilities.

Whenever she saw the three of them like this, Percival couldn't help but feel as if she and they were cut from altogether different kinds of cloth.

"And you, Percival?" Ernest repeated, turning toward her.

"...I'm fine," she answered softly.

"Come on, Percy, there's no need to take everything so seriously. Just relax. Or you could try to be like Leo," Kevin said with a grin as he laid a hand on her shoulder. It was a rather frivolous expression, but Percival could tell that behind that laid-back way of his, he was being serious. Kevin was, perhaps, the most astute member of the team.

"Hey, hold on. What's that supposed to mean?" Lionel demanded, causing Kevin to shirk away.

Percival closed her eyes, trying to calm her racing heart.

Only then did she speak up.

"I am your gun, no more. I will take the sins of destroying your enemies unto myself."

With that, the others all turned toward her.

"I'm tired of hearing that," Laetitia said with a forced smile. "Can't you say something else for once?"

"Agreed," Lionel added with a sigh of resignation.

"You're a strange one sometimes, Percy," Kevin said, nonplussed.

Ernest, however...

"Come now, everyone. There's no need to turn this into an argument."

He, at least, accepted her as she was.

In this team, with these people, she really could bring herself to feel at ease.

It was too much for her.

"Now then, shall we head off?" Ernest asked, glancing at each of them in turn, when there came a knock at the door.

"Now? Right before the match?" Laetitia moaned as she went to unlock it.

It was a stony-faced member of the administrative staff. One of Gallardworth's, judging by the uniform.

"Miss Percival... This... Someone from the institute left it for you..."

"—!"

That name alone was enough to send everyone into a stir.

"What? Right now...?" Laetitia murmured, clearly fighting to hold herself back.

Percival, however, simply stared at the writing on the card. "This is a fake," she said without any hesitation.

"Huh?"

"It must be a prank. Don't worry about it." With that, she flung it into the rubbish bin.

Right. It was a fake. And she knew just who was behind it, to whom that scribble belonged.

It was a sign, one that could only be understood by someone who had grown up *there*.

I always suspected he would try to meddle in my life again. But why now, of all times...?

"Percival, are you sure?" Ernest asked worriedly as he stared into her eyes.

"Yes, it's fine."

That was the truth.

At least for now.

"...All right. We trust you." He nodded.

After a brief pause, he lifted the Runesword above his head as he took command of the team. "In the name of the holy nimbus, symbol of order!"

With this, the four other members all stood at attention, answering in unison: "For Saint Gallardworth!"

Meanwhile, in Miluše's private quarters at Queenvale Academy for Young Ladies—

"Didn't you hear me—? There's no way they won't win!"

"Right, what Miluše said! Ayato Amagiri can't lose!"

"...No, no matter how you look at it, Team Lancelot has the advantage."

"Right, right! Team battles are all about your combined strength! You've already lost if you go out there shorthanded!"

Miluše and Tuulia were practically shouting, their voices overflowing with confidence. Päivi and Monica, on the other hand, looked somewhat sulky.

Then there was Mahulena, caught in the middle of the two sides. "U-um, everyone, why don't we try to calm down a little..."

This was, however, the usual state of business for Rusalka.

If indeed there was something that didn't feel exactly right, it was probably her own presence among them, Sylvia thought as she glanced at each of the band's members in turn as she sipped her tea.

Just yesterday, she had been planning to go to the Sirius Dome in person to cheer Ayato on. That was, until late last night, when she had received a sudden phone call from Ayato.

That in itself was a surprise, but the contents of the call were even more shocking.

Not only had he encountered Ursula—or rather, Varda—she had been acting alongside this Lamina Mortis person. It wasn't at all clear what the two had hoped to achieve, but it was obvious enough that Mortis was after Ayato.

No sooner had she heard Varda's name than Sylvia found herself burning with impatience and frustration. She had wanted to go to Ayato at that very moment to hear everything in detail.

However, the championship was just the following day, and Ayato would need to rest. She didn't lack so much self-control that she could think only about her own wants and desires. In fact, she should have been grateful to him for calling her immediately after talking to the city guard.

And yet, she still couldn't separate the two conflicting sets of emotions. If she was to go to the Sirius Dome and see Ayato, she feared she might find herself doing something that she would later regret.

Which was why she had thought to watch the match with her juniors in Rusalka. Their uncontrollable gaiety would, she hoped, help to bring her own impatience under control.

"Then let's ask Sylvia!" Miluše announced.

The gazes of the five girls all spun toward her, pulling her back into the here and now.

"Huh? Me?"

"Yep! Who do you think will win?" Miluše beamed, leaning forward in excitement. "Don't hold back!

Sylvia didn't even need to think about it. "Team Enfield, of course."

"I knew it! See, see! Sylvia thinks so, too!" Miluše cried out, ecstatic at having found an ally.

"I knew you had an eye for these things!" Tuulia nodded passionately.

Monica and Päivi, on the other hand, were evidently disappointed.

"What?! Really?"

"...You're just basing that off your personal feelings."

"Yep." Sylvia nodded. "That's what my feelings tell me. I mean, it's only natural to believe in the team of the person you love, right?"

"...!"

She paused there, realizing she had been, perhaps, a little too frank. The faces of the five younger girls had all turned scarlet.

As she watched their adorable reactions, Sylvia felt like laughing for the first time all day.

She truly did want Ayato and the others to win—for her as well as for themselves.

In the audience chamber of the Hall of the Yellow Dragon, Alema watched on from behind a nearby pillar, while the members of Team Yellow Dragon—Xiaohui excluded—knelt in front of the seated Xinglou, each staring at the live broadcast from the Sirius Dome projected in the huge air-window before them.

"Hmm... So I take it that your shared opinion is that Gallardworth will win?" Xinglou asked.

"Yes," Hufeng answered, head bowed respectfully. "Kirin Toudou's absence is a major blow and one that can't be solved through strategy alone."

"I see. And you, Alema? You chose Seidoukan?"

"I didn't say they'd win. Even I think Gallardworth's got the advantage here, and yet..." Alema, her interest piqued, put on a self-satisfied grin. "You should have seen the Murakumo take down that Yabuki head. If he can do that again, no one at Gallardworth is going to stop him."

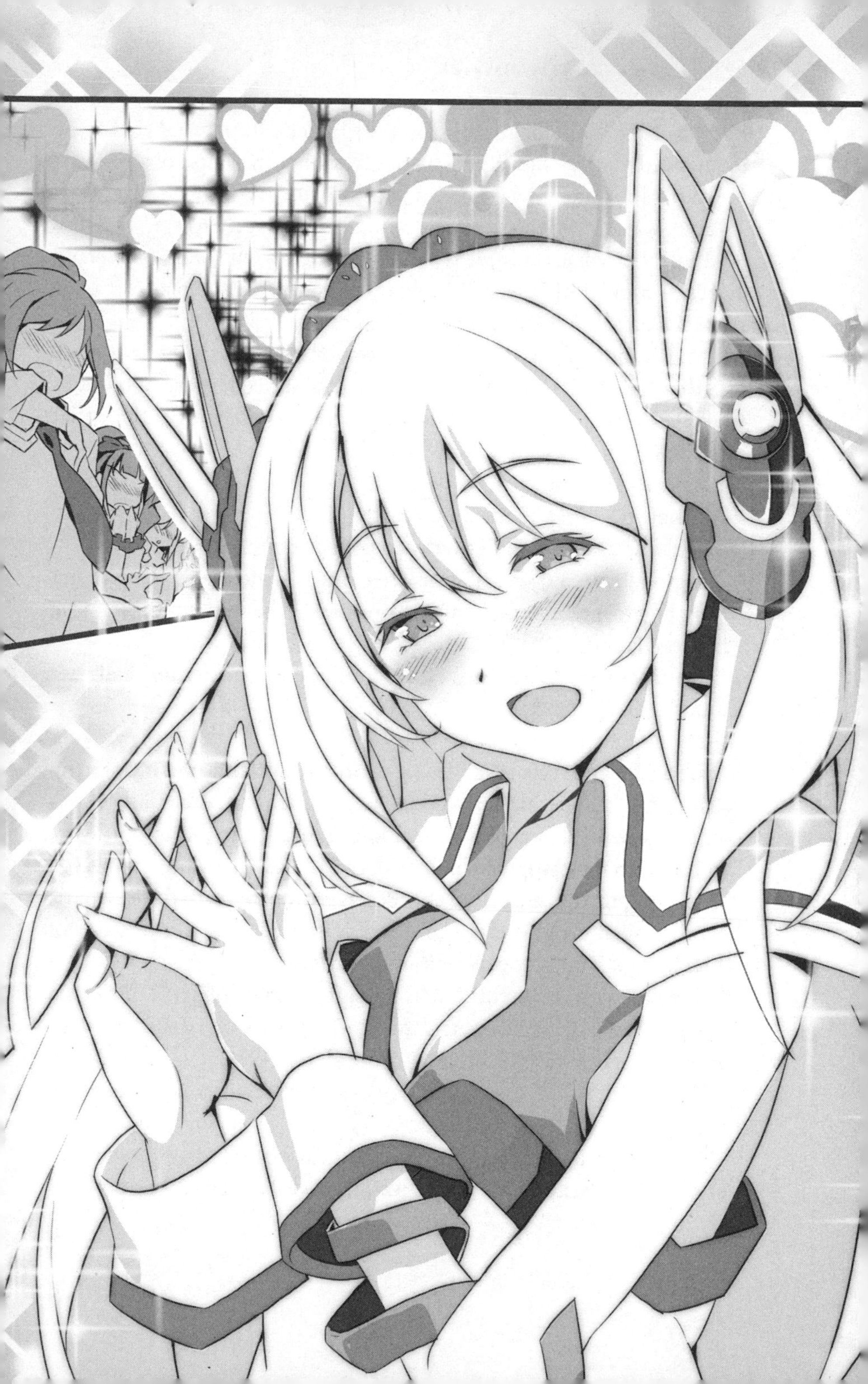

It was clear from his expression that Hufeng didn't find that to be particularly satisfying. "But is he really hiding that kind of strength? He didn't look like it when he was fighting *us*."

"HEY, WATCH IT. ARE YOU SAYING I LIED IN MY REPORT?"

"That's not what I meant. It's just…" Hufeng fell silent, glowering at her. It looked like he still hadn't gotten over his defeat from the previous day.

Xinglou looked down fondly at the two before clapping her hands together lightly. "Now, now. As Alema has noticed, there's no doubt that Ayato Amagiri possesses some hidden power—or rather, that some of it remains sealed away."

"Master, does that mean—"

"—that you think Team Enfield will win?"

The twins asked, completing each other's question.

Xinglou, however, slowly shook her head. "I didn't say that… That would be more of a minimum requirement," she said, trying to stifle a burst of laughter.

Her disciples, kneeling before her, were unable to read her thoughts on the matter.

While at the Le Wolfe Black Institute, most students had little interest in team competitions; a great many uncharacteristically eager students—several dozen of whom had managed to sneak bottles of alcohol onto the campus—had gathered in the quadrangle to watch the championship match of the Festa. Towering air-windows had been installed around the four sides of the wide space, in front of which the gathered crowds waited impatiently.

"Irene, do you really think Mr. Amagiri will be okay…?" Priscilla asked as she struggled to watch the screen from some distance away, a sudden nervousness tightening around her chest.

"It's not gonna be easy," her sister, sitting next to her, answered bluntly.

"Oh…" Priscilla must have realized that herself, deep down, but her sense of gratitude for what Ayato had done for her was perhaps clouding her judgment. Even so, she wanted him to win. She put her hands together to pray for his success.

"Well, there's no way around it. The odds at all the gambling dens are, at least, two-to-one. It doesn't look good when you're a fighter short."

"Hold on. Don't tell me you bet on it?"

"...Ah." Irene looked away as her younger sister trained her gaze upon her.

"I don't believe you, Irene! Mr. Amagiri's been fighting so hard just to get this far! How could you?"

"N-no, that isn't how it went! I mean, I—I was supporting them, like..." Irene waved her hands as if to take back what she had said.

At that moment, however, the atmosphere of the space around them underwent a sudden change.

An uneasy murmur spread among the gathered students, a sense of tension like nothing Priscilla had ever felt before falling over her.

For a second, she had thought she had seen something stir on the other side of the air-window—but no, it was something else.

Shock and terror, disgust and reverence—the air was filled with a potent blend of emotions.

The crowd soon split down the middle as students scrambled to put some distance between themselves and the young woman who had appeared before them. They all knew who that eerie white hair and those ominous red eyes belonged to.

"Orphelia Landlufen..."

That name had come to symbolize the ultimate sense of dread in Le Wolfe—and in all of Asterisk. Two-time champion of the Lindvolus, Le Wolfe's undefeated top-ranked fighter, was said to be the strongest and most feared Strega in all six schools combined.

And she was walking straight toward Priscilla.

But as she stared back at her, what Priscilla saw wasn't someone to cower away from, but rather an individual filled to bursting with sadness and resignation.

And yet, Priscilla's body was completely paralyzed, rendered

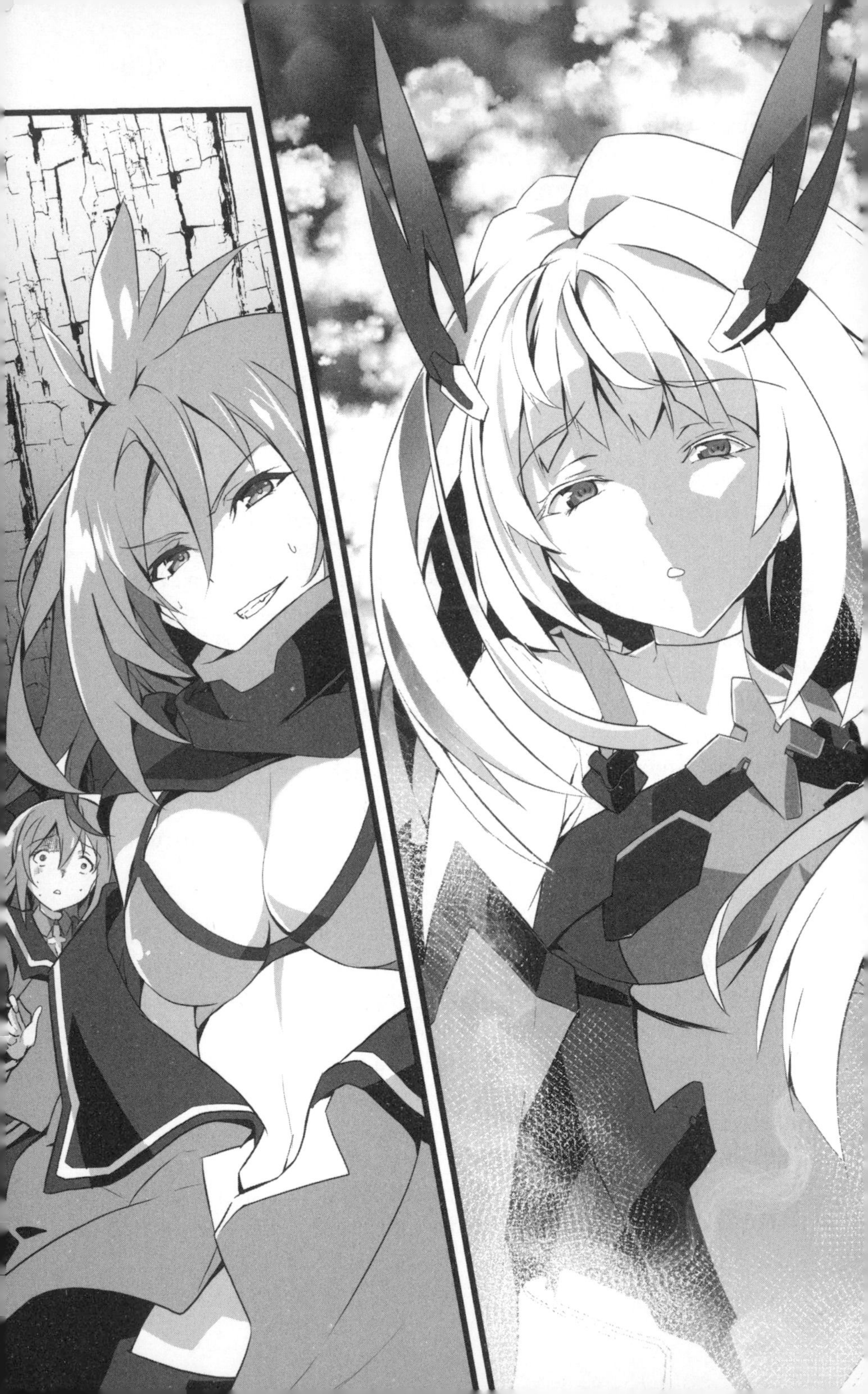

immobile by an instinctive, inescapable sense of despair. Her flesh had turned numb all the way down to her fingers and toes, her throat choking with an unreleased scream.

"Yo, Ereshkigal. Did you want something?" Irene said, stepping forward as if to shield her.

Irene truly did live up to her ranking as Le Wolfe's number three, Priscilla thought with wonder. Even exposed to Orphelia's aura, she was still able to confront her on her feet.

"...Yes. Can we talk?" In spite of her appearance, Orphelia's voice was surprisingly girlish and sweet.

So why... Why is it still so terrifying?

"To talk? With us?"

"Yes. It has to be you."

"Oh...?" Irene raised a doubtful eyebrow before pointing at the nearby air-window with her thumb. "Well, I guess that's fine. Can we do it after the match?"

"...? Ah, the Gryps." Orphelia stared up at the huge air-window, as if she had only now realized what was going on.

Both teams were about to enter the stage of the Sirius Dome.

"All right. When it's finished," Orphelia replied before turning back in the direction from which she had come.

"What? You aren't watching it? Not even the final?"

"...I'm not interested," she said without so much as a backward glance.

She did, however, pause for a brief moment, tilting her gaze ever so slightly toward the overhead air-window.

Team Enfield had just entered the stage from the east gate.

Meanwhile, in Allekant Académie's research facility...

"...She's out again, is she?" Camilla Pareta sighed as she came to a stop in front of Ernesta Kühne's lab. "What on earth could be more important than the match?"

She had thought to invite Ernesta to watch the championship with her, but it looked like she had come in vain.

In fact, Ernesta seemed to be away from the lab a lot lately—or rather, she seemed to be leaving Asterisk itself quite frequently. In the other schools, leaving the city normally required going through a maze of administrative procedures, but at Allekant, which had associated research facilities and factories all over the world, the process was comparatively straightforward. Camilla herself frequently left the city to visit contracted enterprises and research institutes.

But lately, Ernesta's absences had become conspicuous.

Just as Camilla's thoughts had reached this point, however, a woman dressed in a white lab coat and with a somewhat unsteady gait appeared down the corridor. "Oh my, what do we have here? If it isn't our dear Ferrovius head." Hilda Jane Rowlands—or as she was better known at Allekant, Magnum Opus—laughed.

"Who would have thought I would bump into the head of Tenorio here? It's been a while." Camilla would have preferred that it be longer.

Camilla's dislike for Tenorio's disregard for human life and dignity knew no bounds, but her hatred for the woman who represented their way of thinking ran deeper still.

"It has, hasn't it...? Are you here to see Ernesta Kühne as well?"

"Indeed... And you?"

The question hardly needed asking. It was clear enough from the way she had asked it that that had been her intention.

"Oh, it isn't anything major. She seems to be awfully busy these days."

"She does."

"I wonder what she could be doing?" Hilda goaded, breaking out into a dry, rasping laugh.

"Who knows?" Camilla replied offhandedly.

At that, Hilda leaned forward, her expression one of exaggerated surprise. "What's that? Not even you know what your dear friend is up to?"

"...She's in Pygmalion. I'm in Ferrovius. There are things we don't talk about."

Pygmalion and Ferrovius were currently in an alliance of sorts, but that didn't mean they shared all their research. Strictly

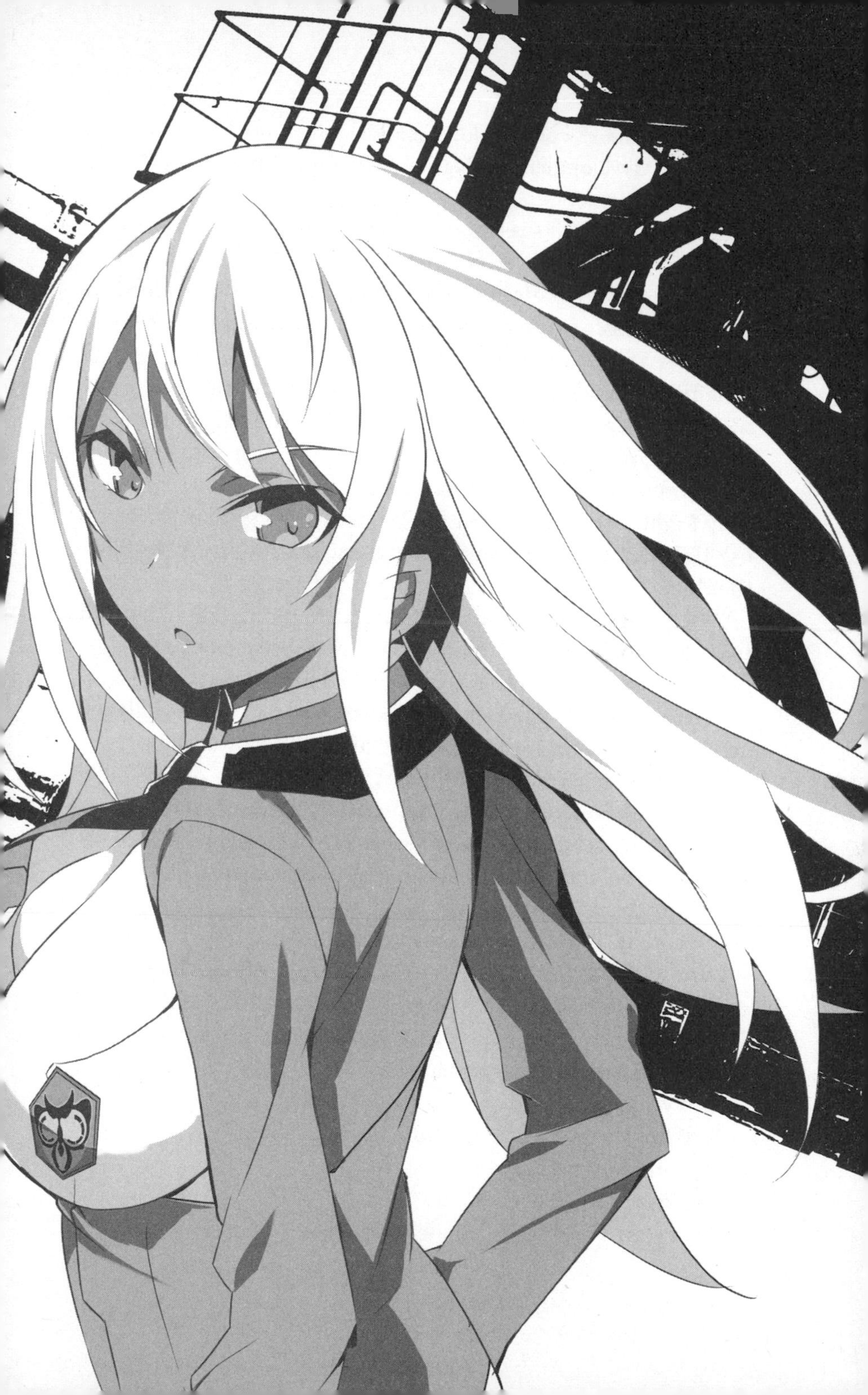

speaking, their cooperation really only involved Ferrovius's continued development of Pygmalion's puppet research to produce practical armaments.

That said, Camilla's relationship with Ernesta on a personal level was something else entirely.

"I see, I see. Do forgive my ignorance," Hilda said in feigned apology, but it was clear from her bearing and expression that her words didn't even run skin-deep.

Camilla should have left it at that, but her frustration boiling over, she found herself remembering something she had heard a short while ago from one of Ferrovius's many intelligence agents. In the end, her curiosity got the better of her.

"...Right, Magnum Opus," she began. "I heard that you tried to use the Murakumo for your own ends, but he gave you the cold shoulder."

"My, you *are* well informed. But you shouldn't talk about it like that. It was only ever going to be a fair trade between equals."

"Oh? My apologies. But it *is* true that he turned you down?"

At this, Hilda shrugged her shoulders, a weird, unnaturally innocent smile plastered on her face. "He did. But that was then."

"...So you haven't given up, I take it?"

Hilda broke out into a fit of laughter. "Why give up now? The main event is only just getting started, after all. He won't have even satisfied the first condition until he wins the tournament."

"So you think Seidoukan will win?"

"Of course," she answered without hesitation.

Camilla could only frown in response. Given their circumstances and the current variables, it would be all but impossible for Team Enfield to defeat Team Lancelot. Camilla had nothing against them personally, but that was an objective fact.

And yet...

"Is there any particular reasoning behind that?"

"No. Just my intuition."

"Hmm..." Camilla fell silent.

"This seems like a good opportunity to let you in on a little secret,"

Hilda continued, her eyes narrowing like a cat's. "It's that sense of intuition that sets people like Ernesta Kühne and me apart from the likes of you, Camilla Pareto. All great scientists are gifted with intuition. We have it. Mediocre researchers like yourself don't."

"...How dare you?!" Camilla scowled back at her, but Hilda didn't seem to pay her any heed.

Camilla was well aware that her own talents didn't reach the level of those belonging to Ernesta or Hilda, but that was just too blunt.

"Ah, the match is about to start. I'm looking forward to it!" Hilda said over her shoulder with a backward wave.

Camilla could do no more than grit her teeth in frustration as she watched her leave.

Finally, at the Sirius Dome—

"*Team Enfield and Team Lancelot are making their way onto the stage! Two hundred and fifty teams have fought to reach this final stage in this year's Gryps, but now only these two remain! Here we are at last—the championship!*"

CHAPTER 7
TEAM LANCELOT

The confident aura emanating from the members of Team Lancelot across the stage was nothing short of overwhelming. And it made sense: Taking into account no more than their individual abilities, it seemed all but impossible for Team Enfield to prevail.

As they faced their five opponents, standing across from them in a row, Ayato couldn't help but feel as if a towering mountain were about to come crashing down upon him.

"Hey, Ayato." At the sound of Julis's whisper, he snapped back to his surroundings.

Amid the thunderous roar of cheering voices, Ernest stepped forth, holding out a hand toward him.

"It's a shame you're one short, but I'm afraid we won't go easy on you."

"I know," Ayato replied, handshake firm.

"Let's give them all a fitting performance," he said with his usual fresh, invigorated voice.

Next, it was Laetitia who stepped forward.

Her gaze was directed not at Ayato, but at Claudia, standing beside him.

"The time has finally come, Claudia. Today's the day I finally pay you back for everything that's happened over the years!" she called out with her typical confidence.

"I'm looking forward to it," Claudia replied with a gentle laugh.

It was clear to Ayato that she was putting her heart and soul into this match in a way she hadn't just a few days prior.

But it wasn't just her. The same went for Saya and Julis, too, not to mention himself.

That was the only interaction between the two teams before the match.

There was nothing more they needed to say. It was a team battle, and they would be facing one another as a group. That was all.

The only thing left to do was wait.

And then—

"Gryps Championship Match—battle start!"

No sooner did it sound than the mechanical voice was drowned out by an excited roar.

Team Lancelot immediately moved into battle formation, their movements perfectly synchronized.

Ernest and Lionel took point in the vanguard, with Laetitia and Kevin falling back to the middle of the stage, and Percival acting as support in the rear—the same formation that they always employed.

On Team Enfield's side, Ayato and Claudia took the vanguard, with Julis slightly behind them as support, while Saya, in the rear, began to charge her Waldenholt Mark II.

"Let's get started!" Laetitia was the first to activate her abilities, summoning a pair of gigantic, semi-translucent wings of light from her back. They unfurled like amber spider's legs as she lunged toward Ayato and Claudia.

"Burst into bloom—*Primrose!*" Next up was Julis, casting nine separate fireballs, each resembling graceful blossoms in a dance-like volley over the top of their heads.

Laetitia's wings swung downward from above, the fireballs unfurling like beautiful flowers as they collided with them, while underneath, Ayato and Ernest, and Claudia and Lionel, rushed to meet one another.

"I've been looking forward to crossing swords with you! And to think we've been given such a grand stage as this! We truly should thank the gods!" Ernest's Lei-Glems clanged against Ayato's Ser Veresta, each impact throwing off sparks in every direction.

While the Lei-Glems had the ability to make physical contact with only that which its user wanted to strike, and the Ser Veresta was capable of burning through everything it touched, when they came together like this, those abilities essentially canceled each other out.

"I hope I can live up to your expectations…!"

In a duel, victory inevitably went to whichever party possessed the greater swordsmanship, and in that area, Ernest was practically flawless.

It only took a brief moment for Ayato to realize what exactly he was up against.

Gallardworth's particular style of swordsmanship was characterized by wide arcing moves and quick flicks of the wrist, but unlike, say, Elliot's, Ernest's was a larger two-handed weapon. That meant he wasn't as fast, but he more than made up for that with technique.

"*Urg…*" Just as Ayato found himself being pushed back, another volley of Julis's primroses fluttered down from above.

Ernest brushed the flames aside, his expression unflinching.

Ayato, taking advantage of that momentary opportunity, rallied himself, dashing forward.

But of course, these were the kinds of moments when a team's support would step in. Just as he was approaching Ernest, three of Laetitia's luminescent wings descended upon him.

He sliced through one of them with the Ser Veresta, the remaining two all but diving onto each other to escape his counterattack, when he heard Claudia's voice, crying out as she parried Lionel's spear.

"Ayato, above!"

"—!"

Ernest, using the two wings that had dived to the ground as a foothold, had leaped high into the air to attack from overhead.

Ayato managed to repel the attack not a moment too late, but only to have Saya call out: "It's coming!"

Glancing across the stage at her warning, he caught sight of Percival at the opposing team's rear, one hand lifted into the air as she intoned solemnly: "*A halo of mercy and atonement I give to thee.*"

Almost instantaneously, the huge chalice-shaped Orga Lux floating above her began to emanate a golden light.

After a short moment, a brilliant current burst out of it as if to sweep away the entire stage, wide and fast enough to engulf everyone in its path, comparable in force even with Saya's most powerful Luxes.

That band of light, the Holy Grail's signature ability, was capable of robbing its targets of consciousness not through brute force, but rather by psychological shock and awe, making it all but impossible to defend against.

In other words, Team Lancelot had two supposedly invulnerable weapons: Ernest's Lei-Glems and Percival's Amalthean Goat.

What was even more astonishing was that each member of Team Lancelot successfully evaded the oncoming wave without even the slightest hint of needing to communicate their actions.

Rather, they had taken advantage of their opponents' momentary lapse in concentration to increase the fervor of their own attacks.

Unlike the Lei-Glems, the Amalthean Goat wasn't capable of directing its abilities at a particular target. Even so, should anyone in its path make a mistake, there was no way that they would be able to properly defend themselves.

Fortunately, thanks to Saya's swift support, Ayato was able to leap to safety, but he knew now not to let down his guard.

I guess I'm going to need to rely on shiki *here…*

Using the Amagiri Shinmei style's perception-expanding technique, he would be able to have a faster, more accurate grasp of everything happening on the stage.

The downside, as pointed out by his homeroom teacher, Kyouko, during their special training sessions over the past months, was that by shifting his attention to his surroundings, he might not be able to react properly to what was happening directly in front of him.

This could be a bad idea against him…

Ernest's swordsmanship was so faultless, revealing not a single opening or weakness, that, to the outside observer, it must have resembled a graceful dance more than it did fierce combat.

Ayato caught his breath as he prepared himself to meet him head-on.

"Boom."

No sooner had Percival unleashed her wide-range attack with the Amalthean Goat than Saya unleashed a volley from her Waldenholt Mark II homing blaster.

Each burst homed in precisely on the school crests of Team Lancelot's five members, and each was then casually brushed aside by their target's weapon of choice.

But that didn't matter, because Saya's role this time was twofold.

Her first responsibility was to support the other three members of the team and to prevent the vanguard from collapsing under the opposing team's attacks.

The second was to monitor Percival in Team Lancelot's rearguard—or rather, to monitor the Amalthean Goat—and to make sure that the others knew when she was about to use it.

Based on her calculations using the available data, the Orga Lux's charging time was ninety-nine seconds—significantly longer than her own Waldenholt. That meant she should have little difficulty covering those attacks.

During that charging time, Saya pulled her two favorite handgun-shaped Luxes from the Waldenholt's oversized back unit. She didn't have a second to waste.

She quickly adjusted the Waldenholt's recoil-control vernier, using it to unleash a volley of covering fire toward Ayato and Claudia.

Percival, meanwhile, had activated a revolver-shaped Lux of her own.

They each lifted their weapons as their gazes locked.

"—!"

"…!"

Bullets of light passed in front of her at high speed, just as her own cross fire forced Percival to dive to the ground.

The two glared at each other in silence before simultaneously shifting their attention to their respective teams.

Phew... She's got good aim.

Saya couldn't help but be impressed. Her opponent's skill with a gun was of the highest class. Even without her Orga Lux, she would no doubt make a formidable opponent. On top of that, she had the objectivity, quick decision-making aptitude, and above all, composure necessary for someone in the rearguard.

Saya couldn't help but be reminded of Rimcy, but in a way, it was Percival who was the more puppetlike of the two.

It was as if she had freed herself of all redundant thoughts and emotions, becoming a cold, inanimate weapon in and of herself.

"—Hah...!"

At that moment, Laetitia's brilliant wings dashed toward her, forcing her to quickly adjust the trajectory of her homing attacks.

Unlike Team Yellow Dragon, whose members tended to engage their chosen targets individually, Team Lancelot operated as a cohesive unit, meaning that, barring some kind of unexpected development, the rearguard was unlikely to come under fire from the opposing vanguard.

Which meant that she could focus on keeping Laetitia at bay while also exchanging fire with Percival.

However, that was easier said than done.

How long can I keep this up...?

Even putting aside Kirin's absence, their combined strength as a team still didn't quite match that of their opponents.

They had been able to hold out thus far, but the longer the match drew out, the closer they came to losing control.

On top of that, she couldn't keep using the Waldenholt indefinitely. Her Luxes resembled Meteor Arts in more than a few ways, chief among them being that they consumed a lot of prana.

She paused there, glancing up in a hurry.

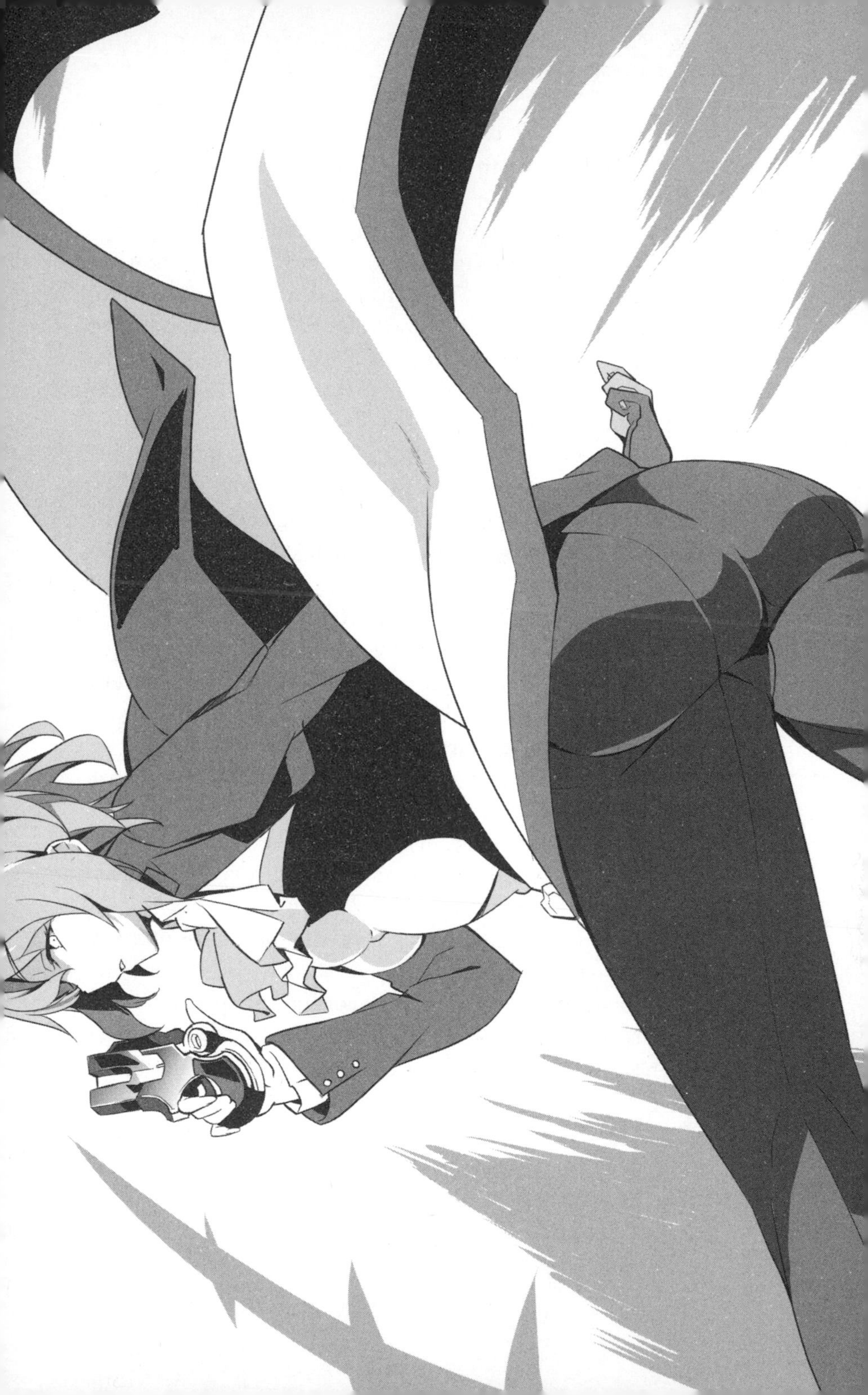

"—The second wave! Watch out!" she called out, just as another flood of golden light began to spill out of the Amalthean Goat.

A burst of light passed over Julis's ducked head.

She had managed to dodge this first attack, but Kevin, who had leaped upon one of Laetitia's outstretched wings to escape from it himself, now came descending toward her with sword outdrawn.

She brought around the three remaining units of her Rect Lux to meet his attack, but Kevin deftly maneuvered his huge black shield to brush them all aside.

His alias, Gareth the Black Shield, wasn't just for show.

In contrast to his extravagant appearance and frivolous personality, his fighting style was particularly slow and cautious.

"Splendid, Glühen Rose! What an ardent attack! What do you say, won't you join me for dinner one of these days?"

"I'm afraid I'm just not interested in dandies!" Julis called back, a lance of flame taking shape as she waved her rapier through the air—her *Longiflorum* technique manifesting at point-blank range.

"Whoa…! That's a shame!" he responded as he parried it with his sword, before rushing forward to slam her with his shield.

Julis grimaced as the impact threw her backward, but she wasted no time before climbing back to her feet.

"It looks like the princess prefers straitlaced guys like you, Leo!"

Julis jumped backward as Lionel's keen-edged great spear shot in front of her.

"This is no time for banter, Kevin! We're in the middle of a match!"

So that shield bash was a diversion…

She wouldn't have time to dodge the oncoming spear.

She concentrated her prana on defense, but just before it could reach her, two swords flashed in front of her to brush it away.

"Claudia!"

"Julis, cover me!"

Taking note of Laetitia's brilliant wings, again about to come crashing down from above, Julis activated her trap.

"Burst into bloom—*Epiphyllum!*"

A huge orchard-shaped flower appeared over their heads, holding Laetitia's wings at bay.

And just in time, too.

She didn't have time to relax, however, as Kevin and Lionel were closing in on her and Claudia from either side.

"I'm sorry about this, but we're not going to let up!"

Julis and Claudia stood back-to-back, ready to meet the two oncoming young men with her recalled Rect Lux units and the Pan-Dora, respectively.

Their two opponents rushed them in an attempt to catch them in a pincer move.

"*Urg...!* What do we do, Claudia?!" Julis cried out. "This is going from bad to worse!"

"Even so, we can't afford to lose another one of us...! We're just going to have to keep going!" she called back through clenched teeth, when all of a sudden, the Pan-Dora began to glow.

As Lionel's spear rose high into the air, Claudia pushed herself off from Julis's back, catching Kevin's blade between her own twin swords.

Her movements were as graceful and deliberate as those of an acrobat.

She must be using the Pan-Dora's precognition!

But she couldn't have had much stock left.

"Burst into bloom—*Livingston Daisy!*"

Like Claudia had said, all they could do was keep going.

Julis put the vast majority of her technique into covering her and holding Laetitia in check. After all, if even one of them was defeated, the rest would soon follow.

Julis's role, as the team's support, was to assist both the vanguard and the rearguard—in other words, to ensure that the team could keep operating as a whole.

"Claudia, now!"

"I know...!"

She boosted her prana, focusing her attention on controlling both the spiraling flames of her Livingston Daisy technique and the three units of her Rect Lux.

*   *   *

"Ugh...!" Claudia managed, somehow, to stop Lionel's spear by catching it between her twin blades.

Julis intensified the power of her technique in an attempt to support her, but Kevin immediately moved to intercept it.

These two make for an unpleasant combination!

Lionel's and Kevin's combat styles couldn't be more different, and yet, fighting together, their coordination was odiously precise. Lionel's spear had both a long reach and a significant strength behind it, making him the perfect choice for blocking an opponent's counterattacks, and was all the more terrifying given that the coarseness of his style was nonetheless without flaw.

Kevin, on the other hand, was focusing on landing a steady stream of attacks with his greatsword and shield before breaking away to safety, but he was so precisely in sync with Lionel that she couldn't capitalize on those openings.

And most vexing of all—

"There's more where that came from!"

Along with that cry came three brilliant wings, forcing her to dodge out of their path while at the same time trying to stick close to Julis.

Distance meant nothing to those wings of light.

Team Lancelot's entire strategy was based, it seemed, on the careful integration of offense and defense.

If, somehow, she could take Laetitia out of the equation, they might have a chance at victory.

But I won't get close to her like this...

Kevin, the opposing team's support, moved perfectly, quickly correcting himself whenever he came close to slipping out of formation. On top of that, Laetitia wasn't the kind of Strega who was too reliant on her abilities. Even if Claudia was to engage her in close combat, she was the kind of fighter who could stand her ground.

In the previous Gryps, there had been several minor weaknesses in her stance, but she looked to have improved considerably since then.

Even if Claudia could face her individually, it wasn't a sure thing that she would come out on top.

All in all, in terms of their members, Team Lancelot and Team Enfield were very similarly structured.

Both teams had their own skilled swordsman armed with an Orga Lux, a rearguard that took time to prepare its moves but was capable of annihilating its targets if they scored a direct hit, and versatile supports skilled in both offense and defense.

Which left them with only one major distinguishing factor.

In other words, Claudia.

Her original reason for fighting in the tournament might have been made irrelevant with the events of the previous days. But after all, she was the one who had invited the others to join her in the first place, so she had a responsibility toward them to do everything she could.

"—!"

At that moment, Percival fired off a barrage of bullets of light toward her.

She threw her body out of their path but found herself coming face-to-face with Lionel. Laetitia's luminescent wings closed in behind her, cutting off any route of escape.

Finding herself caught in a desperate situation, she wasted no time before activating the Pan-Dora's precognition to search for a way out.

She only had twenty seconds of stock left.

She hadn't wanted to spend more than thirty seconds of that stock in the battle against Team Yellow Dragon, but there was no point complaining about it now. She would just have to be frugal.

As she poured her prana into the Orga Lux, the world became drained of color.

It looks like Julis is holding Kevin down, so that leaves…

She began to peer into the future, when a more pressing concern reared its head.

"I suppose this isn't the time to be stingy…!"

Seeing no other alternative, she ended up burning most of her remaining stock.

When her surroundings burst into color and motion, she wove her way past both Lionel's spear and Laetitia's wings of light—all but soaring across the stage as she readied the Pan-Dora to strike.

By the time Ayato recognized his mistake, it was already too late.

Ernest had struck out with a low thrust with the Lei-Glems but quickly followed through with a much deeper attack. As he tried to leap over it, the white blade passed through his shins.

The first thrust had been no more than a feint—his real goal was no doubt to upset his footing.

The Lei-Glems, with its ability to make physical contact only with its intended target, gouged straight through the ground beneath him, sending cracks and fissures spreading out in every direction.

"Agh…!" Ayato tried to brace himself as he landed but ended up losing his balance, just as the glint of Ernest's blade came rushing toward him.

Before it could reach him, however, Claudia came flying out of nowhere, laying into Ernest with a surprise attack, causing him to come to a sudden halt as he turned to meet her.

That was the opening that Ayato needed to correct his posture before rushing to Claudia's aid.

"Thanks, Claudia!"

"Not at all…! But I should warn you that I've used up most of my stock!"

The two, now with a numerical advantage, struck Ernest with everything they had. Their opponent's defense, however, was formidable, while he was clearly concentrating his counterattacks on Claudia.

"Ugh…!" Being an Orga Lux, the Pan-Dora was immune to the Lei-Glems's filtration ability and capable of resisting his attacks, but the difference in skill between their two users was obvious.

Claudia, realizing she couldn't hold out against him, backed away.

"My apologies, Miss Enfield!" Ernest said with a laugh. "But I don't think you're quite fit to take me on."

"...I don't need to be told that, Ernest."

"Claudia, I can handle it from here!" Ayato called after her. "Please help Julis!"

She continued to glare after Ernest for a short moment but soon seemed to remember her role in the match and sped off to support Julis.

"Now then, let's get back to it!" Ernest grinned, launching into yet another fierce attack.

He held his glimmering blade upright and, the next second, thrust it directly toward Ayato's chest. No sooner did Ayato dodge it than he came again from below, along with joint ranged attacks from both Percival and Laetitia. It took every ounce of his concentration just to pull through unscathed.

"Haaah...haaah...!"

Sensing an opportunity, he lashed out with a powerful strike of his own, forcing Ernest to retreat backward.

Neither chased after the other, each staring at their opponent as they evaluated their next move.

Ayato's breathing was ragged. Without letting down his guard, both hands gripped tightly around the hilt, he raised the Ser Veresta upward, all but pointing it directly into the sky.

Ernest, on the other hand, didn't appear even the slightest bit perturbed. It was obvious to anyone who looked that he would hold out long after Ayato was driven to exhaustion.

Nor could anyone mistake the difference in ability between the two.

Ernest was strong.

If the only thing that mattered was raw power, then Xiaohui, armed with his *seisenjutsu*, would no doubt come out on top—but in any real contest, Ernest, thanks to his expert swordsmanship and Orga Lux, would likely be insurmountable, even for him.

"Ah... Very impressive, Ayato." Ernest laughed, invigorated.

Ayato couldn't stop himself from asking a question of his own. "I've been wondering this for a while now... Why do you think so highly of me?"

Xinglou was somewhat similar in that respect, but from his own perspective, both of them seemed to be overestimating him.

At this, Ernest looked back at him in surprise for a second before rushing him with blade lowered.

"Isn't it obvious? You have something that makes me want to challenge you, as a swordsman!"

"What's that...supposed to mean?!"

Ayato blocked the blade tip from reaching his chest, but the most formidable part of Ernest's technique—how he would turn that lunge into first one arcing slash, then another—was yet to come. It was similar, at least at a superficial level, to the Toudou style's Conjoined Cranes, but whereas that technique was based on a thorough mastery of its individual forms, Ernest's skill was such that he seemed to be creating new forms to drive into every available weakness.

"Ha-ha! Yes...I suppose that isn't a particularly convincing response!"

Ayato desperately tried to keep his legs from giving way as he used the base of the Ser Veresta to block an oncoming strike aimed directly at his torso.

"So let me rephrase it! You're my ideal opponent!"

"Ideal...?!" Ayato parroted as he blocked an oncoming thrust from above, their swords locking together.

He might not have had the same amount of physical strength as Ernest, but he wasn't so weak as to allow himself to be pushed over.

"There's something inside you, something dreadful. You're able to hold it back, thanks to your training and sheer willpower, but I can see it... You're *just like me!*"

"—!"

Colorless sparks danced around them as the Lei-Glems clashed against the Ser Veresta.

"And yet, you're fighting so freely, wielding that sword as if nothing holds you back. To tell you the truth, I'm a little jealous...!"

Ernest's eyes began to burn with a powerful flame.

A sudden chill ran down Ayato's spine, and he jumped backward to escape.

Just as he did, Ernest's gleaming sword sliced through the air where he had been standing.

He can do that just by twisting his body and turning his wrist?!

"Unlike yours," Ernest said as his blade carved through the air, "my techniques unfortunately don't have names... But they're rather effective, don't you think?"

Ayato felt his flesh turn cold as something inside him began to writhe.

It was the still-incomplete key he had used to release his power, albeit briefly, when he had fought against Bujinsai.

At the time, the key had still needed more, but he could see it now. It had almost taken shape.

All it needed was a little more...

When—

"Ayato! The third wave!" he heard Saya calling out.

Ayato moved to throw himself to safety as Percival's Amalthean Goat released a flood of golden light, but Laetitia's brilliant wings emerged from the ground to block his path.

"Uh-oh..."

Thanks to his heightened senses having entered the state of *shiki*, he didn't need to look up to know that those wings had managed to box him in.

He would have no difficulty carving an opening with the Ser Veresta—the only question was whether he could do it before the flood reached him.

Which left only one thing to do.

With a tremendous roar, he swung the Ser Veresta downward, cutting straight through the wave of golden light.

That light might indeed have been capable of robbing its target of consciousness should it make contact with them, but the Ser Veresta, Ayato judged, would nonetheless be able to cut through that ability, just like it had the Gravisheath's.

Even so, the Amalthean Goat was more powerful than he had been expecting.

He couldn't tell whether it was the Orga Lux itself that was so powerful or whether Percival was simply that good at channeling it. In either case, the Ser Veresta managed, somehow, to divide the flood, but Ayato had to brace himself lest the force of the torrent send him tumbling and swallow him whole.

All the while, the Ser Veresta, as if urging him to hurry, was demanding yet more prana.

Sorry, but I need you to hang in there...!

It was over in just a few seconds. Even so, he had poured so much prana into withstanding the rush that it had felt like an eternity.

"Now then—my apologies, but I think it's time to finish this!" called Ernest, having circled around to his right as he lunged forward.

Don't tell me...?!

It was a strategy that Ayato himself had used only once before.

Ernest was directing the Lei-Glems not toward him, but at the Ser Veresta.

Both weapons were, of course, Orga Luxes, and so, in principle, neither should have had the power to destroy the other. Yet, in its current state, having exhausted so much energy defending against the Amalthean Goat, the Ser Veresta was significantly weakened.

Ernest, too, must have realized that.

The second that pure-white blade came into contact with the body of the Ser Veresta, a shrill, earsplitting shriek coursed through Ayato's head. He had felt the thoughts and desires of the Orga Lux on numerous occasions in the past, but never before had he experienced anything like this.

Cracks coursed through its exterior, its urm-manadite core losing its luster.

"Ser Veresta...!" Ayato called out, when its blade suddenly melted away.

"Ayato! Get back!" Julis cried as she came flying down on a pair of fiery wings, weapon drawn.

"No, you don't!"

"Ah!"

Laetitia's glowing wings launched toward her from the side, sending her crashing to the ground.

"Now then, you can't stop this empty-handed!" Ernest shouted as he struck.

"—!"

He put his whole body into the attack. His timing was so perfect, as was his speed, that no one in their right mind could have even hoped to dodge it.

And yet, at that moment, Ayato felt something inside him snap open with a click.

*

"…Hmm. It's about time." Madiath, watching the match from the Sirius Dome's special observation lounge, let out a satisfied sigh.

His Lamina Mortis mask lay strewn casually on the desk beside him.

"It looks like it was worth giving him that little extra push last night, after all."

"What does that mean?" Varda, sitting beside him, tilted her head in his direction. "What does this have to do with that?"

"There are three parts to the seal that Haruka placed upon our friend Ayato Amagiri, each of them lifting only when certain conditions are cleared."

"…What's the point of something like that?"

"My guess would be that she had her own way of showing her love for him. But if you really want to know, you'll have to ask her yourself," Madiath continued with a shrug. "Anyway, it seems that the third seal could only be released when his accumulated strength exceeded her own. In other words, it looks like he's finally overtaken her."

"His strength…?" Varda repeated, clearly not yet comprehending.

"There's no need to think that hard about it. It basically just means that he had to reach a certain level in ability."

Varda stared at him with something bordering on disgust. "Don't tell me... So last night was all about tempering his skills?"

"Exactly. That's the quickest way to build up someone's strength, don't you think?" Madiath murmured, the corners of his lips curling in a faint smile. "Now then, let's see if you were worth the effort... Ayato Amagiri."

CHAPTER 8
TEAM ENFIELD

Ayato was staring down at another him in the middle of the darkness.

It was the him who had been sealed away by his sister's ability.

There were three locks attached to the chains that bound his body. The first lay broken, and the second was already unlocked.

As for the third one—as he gazed down at it, he slowly unclenched his hand, revealing a glimmering key.

Unlike last time, this time, the key was complete.

He inserted it into the lock; with a faint echo though the darkness, it sprung open.

As it did, a tremendous force seemed to lift up out of his body, trembling like a living thing, before soaring off into the void.

Only then did he realize—or rather, only then could he clearly recognize—what *it* was.

It wasn't Ayato himself who had been sealed away.

It was the Ayato of the past, of six years prior, who had parted with his sister.

The young Ayato, wearing a carefree smile, held out his hand.

The Ayato of now took it in his own—and as he did so, the darkness around them erupted into dazzling light.

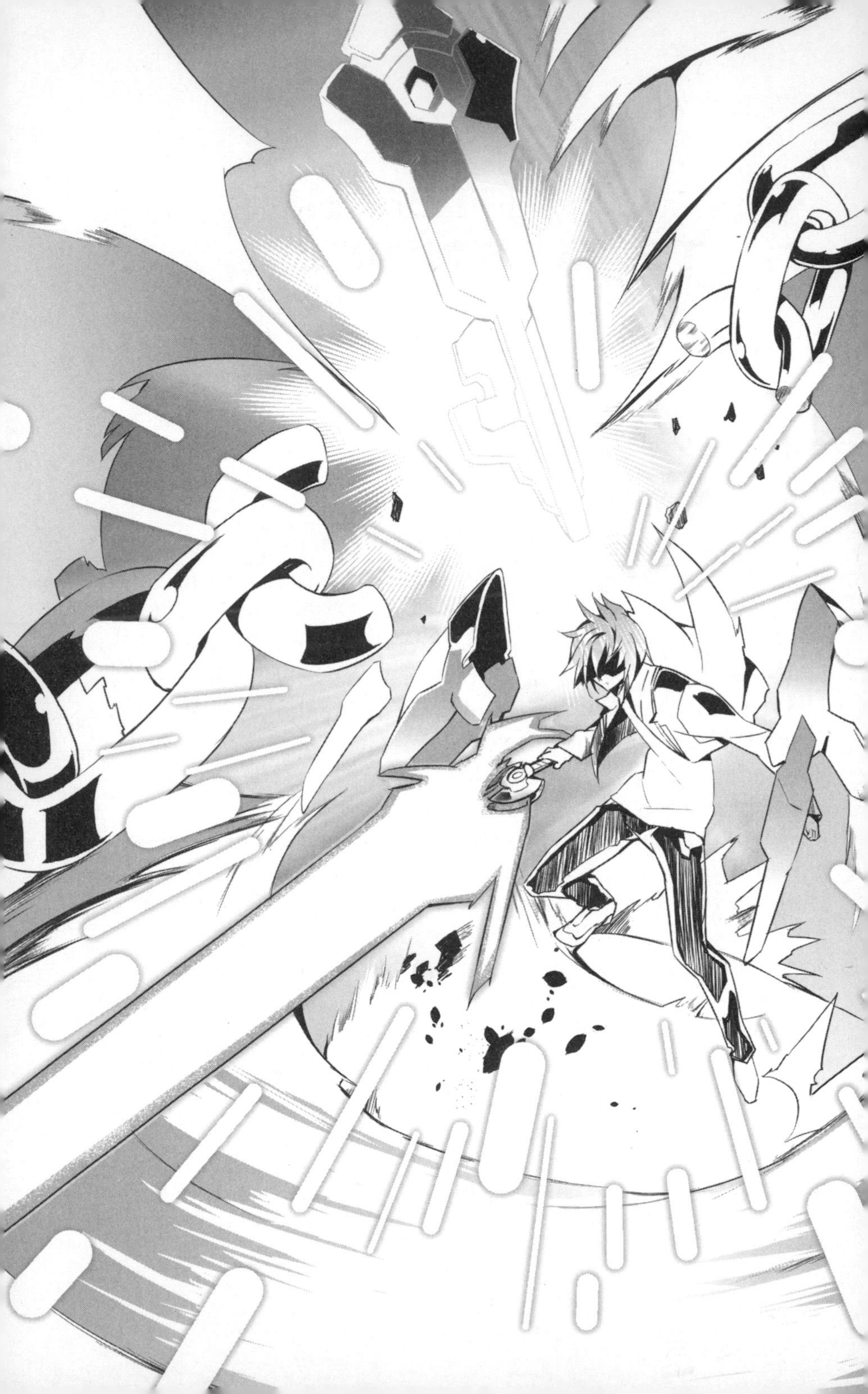

*　　*　　*

"What…?!" Ernest's eyes opened wide in shock.

Ayato could hardly blame him.

His opponent's attack had been timed perfectly, making it all but impossible to evade.

And yet, Ayato had done precisely that.

He crouched down and stepped backward, pulling out his spare blade-type Lux from its holder at his waist.

Ernest's expression changed from one of startle to pure joy.

"Amazing…!" he said as he resumed his fighting posture before, once again, stepping forward.

First, he thrust his blade low toward the ground, following through with an upward arc.

With his current Lux, blocking Ernest's Lei-Glems simply wouldn't be possible.

Even so, Ayato dodged his consecutive strikes with minimal movement.

"Hmm…"

He felt like he had when he had fought Bujinsai, as if he had returned to who he was meant to be.

He could feel the energy flowing through every corner of him, as if his mind and body had melted together and become one.

He slashed upward with his blade, twisting his wrist as he did so to flow immediately into a diagonal downward slash. Ernest attempted to raise the Lei-Glems to defend himself but wasn't able to prevent the second part of the attack from cutting through his uniform.

"—!"

Ernest hadn't made a mistake.

Ayato had simply been too fast.

His body was moving much more naturally, precisely, and above all, faster than ever before.

"Ernest!"

Four additional luminescent wings had sprung from Laetitia's back, making for twelve in total that were now rushing toward him.

But catching his breath, Ayato then sliced through them all with a single flash of his blade.

"How is that...?!"

Even so, Team Lancelot's coordination was nothing short of incredible. In the brief span of time that it had taken him to destroy those glowing wings, Kevin and Lionel had appeared out of nowhere to catch him in the middle of a pincer formation.

Glancing across the stage, he could see that the only thing stopping Percival from joining in on the attack was Claudia.

"Impressive! But without your Ser Veresta, you're ours!"

"En garde!"

The two launched into a combination move, coming at him in the blink of an eye with both sword and spear.

Ayato, however, turned aside the long blade with a casual flick of his body, while at the same time parrying the spear descending toward him from above with what must have looked like no more than a gentle caress.

With that out of the way, he then followed through with an attack of his own.

Kevin managed to raise his shield to deflect the full force of the strike, but Lionel, armed only with his two-handed greatsword, had no way of parrying it.

"Lionel Karsch—crest broken."

"Wait... What?"

The tip of Ayato's blade had cut straight through his school crest.

Lionel's eyes opened wide in astonishment before he fell to his knees with a silent thud.

Ayato, however, paid him little attention as he focused on launching another strike aimed for Kevin.

"You've got to be kidding me...! That was... Even Ernest couldn't do that...!"

Gallardworth's students prided themselves on their sturdiness in battle, so Kevin's defensive techniques were as excellent as could have been expected.

But even so—

"Amagiri Shinmei Style Master Technique—*Hornet Charge!*"

Ayato took a short step backward to gauge his timing before twisting his body and diving forward to unleash the attack.

Kevin's shield began to crack under the force of the repeated thrusts, until it finally shattered.

Ayato stepped forward once again, this time aiming for his school crest, when—

"Even I couldn't do *what*, exactly?"

Ernest inserted himself into the fray, deftly brushing aside Ayato's blade.

"Kevin, go see to Miss Enfield! Percival is probably nearing her limit!"

"A-ah... Understood!"

Ayato let him go, turning his gaze toward Ernest—when he was overcome by some inexplicable sense of unease.

There was something different about his opponent's stance. Gallardworth's style of combat normally centered on maintaining a balance between offense and defense, but the way that Ernest was holding the Lei-Glems suggested he was focusing now purely on attack.

And there was something else, too.

"Now then, shall we continue?" As he spoke, his usual composed smile fell away, revealing a disquieting grin.

"...Julis, are you okay?"

"Ah, sorry!"

As a barrage of Laetitia's wings of light pummeled into her, one had managed to score a hit on Julis's leg. Fortunately, with Saya's help, she had been able to drive away the pursuit, but there was no hiding the fact that she was injured.

Laetitia's wings continued to sweep down to check their every movement, but Saya, though burdened with helping her and still with the vernier of the Waldenholt fully equipped, slid past them all as she made her way across the stage.

Julis couldn't say that she liked being put in this situation, but right now, she had no choice but to rely on her.

She could probably still use her *Strelitzia* technique to fly across the stage, but in the air, she would make an easy target for Laetitia's ever-transforming wings.

"Anyway… When did Ayato get so strong?"

As she summoned up a ring of fire to help defend Claudia from Kevin, she could do little but watch out of the corner of her eye in worry as he exchanged strikes against Ernest.

There could be no mistaking that, until just a short moment ago, Ernest had had the advantage.

That was to be expected—not only was he considered Asterisk's premier swordsman, he was widely regarded as one of the greatest, if not *the* greatest of their age.

And yet now, the situation seemed to have been reversed.

No matter how you looked at it, amid the furious exchange of blows, Ayato was the one who had Ernest on his toes.

On top of that, Ayato wasn't even wielding the Ser Veresta. If he still had the Orga Lux, the battle might already have been over.

Ayato was practically overwhelming him.

She had heard from Claudia about how he had driven Yabuki's father back, but to think that he could be this powerful…

"…He must have completely broken the seal that Haru placed on him. In other words, that's his real strength." Saya's voice, as she exchanged fire with Percival, was low, but it held an unmistakable touch of pride.

"I can see that… I just had no idea he could be *this* strong…"

"Do you remember what I told you a while ago? That if you really fought Ayato, you wouldn't be in one piece?"

"…Ah, I remember. It was when we were showing him around the campus, right?"

At the time, she had thought Saya was merely trying to provoke her.

"I always thought it was strange. If the Ayato I remembered had kept growing, he'd have to be really, really strong—like Haru was. He was still strong when he broke his seal, but not as strong as I had been expecting."

"What?!"

Saya spun around sharply to dodge an oncoming attack from Laetitia aimed at her blind spot, Julis clinging to her to avoid being thrown off.

"It might have made sense if he had given up on his training and stopped practicing, but that doesn't look like it was the case," Saya continued softly between carefully timed shots with her handgun. "When he came here, he was really trying to do his best, so he must have stayed at it after I moved away."

"What are you trying to say?"

"...Haven't you noticed? It's been more than a year since Ayato first arrived here, *but he hasn't really gotten any stronger* since then."

"What...?" Aghast, Julis stared back at her. "N-n-not at all! I mean, he's..." But she stopped there, unable to properly refute her.

Now that she mentioned it, the only time she had really felt a significant increase in Ayato's strength was whenever he broke his seal. That was in spite of the countless hours that they had spent training together since the Phoenix.

"He was still able to pick up new techniques, like our coordination patterns, but he didn't really move beyond that... But his real power, the Ayato that I'd always known, has probably been held back by Haru's seal all this time."

"I-impossible! If that's true..." Julis stared at Ayato in shock.

Haruka had placed that seal on him six years ago. In which case—

"Right. That power has been building up in him for six years now. He should be able to win no matter who he faces," Saya declared, brimming with confidence.

Across the stage, a sudden flash of Ayato's sword seemed to send the Lei-Glems flying from Ernest's hand—

No, wait... He threw it away himself?

Julis had to strain her eyes to make out what was going on.

This time, it was Ernest's turn to undergo a transformation of his own.

*

Ernest Fairclough was the kind of person who kept himself under control at all times.

Even if it wasn't what he himself truly wanted to do, if, by doing so, he could bring some kind of benefit to his friends, his house, his school—indeed, to all those around him—then that was good enough for him.

This wasn't to say that he was particularly philanthropic or altruistic at heart. Rather, if, by acting selfishly, one was to cause disadvantage to befall others, then it was simply more efficient to take the total sum of consequences into account and act accordingly. That was the most logical way to survive in this world under the thumb of the integrated enterprise foundations.

It was, of course, stifling to live while having all but suffocated his heart, but Ernest excelled at deceiving even himself. That allowed him to keep breathing, and he didn't feel any particular discomfort or difficulty as a result of it. Except, perhaps, when it came to what had happened with *her*.

But that was a long time ago now.

And it wasn't as if he hadn't sensed this moment coming.

That way of living would break down the moment he wished for something that was difficult to change.

Even if he had thrown everything else away, even if he cast aside everything that he had so painstakingly built up until now, there was one wish he needed to see come true.

He feared it, somewhere deep inside himself, and yet, at the same time, he was desperately searching for it.

"Haaah!"

"Argh!"

He warded away Ayato's oncoming strike at his school crest with the Lei-Glems, but his opponent immediately adjusted the course of his movements and swooped down with another strike.

Ayato Amagiri.

His swordsmanship and movements—practically his whole fighting style—were completely different from just a brief moment ago.

Their most essential components, however, remained unchanged. It was more like the gears had clicked into place, his technique becoming clearer and more precise.

Even with the overwhelming advantage of the Lei-Glems, Ernest was still being one-sidedly pushed back.

At this rate, it was only a matter of time before his school crest was destroyed.

"Ha-ha… Ha-ha-ha…!" The situation was getting out of hand, but still, he couldn't hold back his mirth.

He couldn't help but be overjoyed by this adversity and by the one who had plunged him into it.

There was a craving deep inside him, something he couldn't oppose.

He had felt it, intuitively, the moment he had first set eyes upon this opponent.

Ayato was just like himself.

There was a wickedness inside his opponent, something that he kept under control at all times.

And yet, that opponent was far freer that he himself was. It would be a lie to say that he wasn't jealous—but that was hardly important.

What mattered now was that that opponent—Ayato Amagiri—was closing in on him.

Then so be it.

In that case, there was no need to keep putting up with it any longer.

He would acknowledge that craving, his impossible wish for change, for which he was willing to sacrifice anything and everything to have granted.

He would unleash the power that he himself was keeping in check.

"What are you...?" Ayato stared at him in surprise as he cast the Lei-Glems aside.

Right. He didn't care what happened next.

Whether it was the gloomy, stifling Fairclough house; the excessive expectations and demands disguised as flattery of the people around him; the worthless Runesword that forced him to bury his true self; the alias Pendragon that hung heavy around his neck; the lip service and empty loyalty of the academy that purported to care about him; his companions bound to him through respect and friendship; his foolish, charming, courageous sister, so filled with self-reproach and dedication that she was willing to throw herself into the heat of battle for him; and then after, his memories of *her*—now that it had come to this, none of it mattered anymore.

He activated the longsword-type Lux that he had been keeping in reserve and, for the first time in his life, felt a grin—a real, authentic grin—rising up from the depths of his heart.

*

Ayato knew, on some instinctive level, to fall back.

At that moment, a fierce slash, aimed directly at his neck, brushed against the edge of his skin.

It wasn't the kind of graceful arc that characterized Gallardworth's style of swordsmanship—it was more direct than that, sharper, neither elegant nor showy, a technique designed to achieve nothing more than to slaughter one's opponent.

"...Is that the real you, Ernest Fairclough?"

"Indeed. The real me to match the real you."

Casually lowering his sword, Ernest's ever-handsome face now looked somewhat distorted. He directed a fiendish grin toward Ayato—one that looked, somehow, strangely familiar.

"Yaaaaaargh!"

"Raaaaaah!"

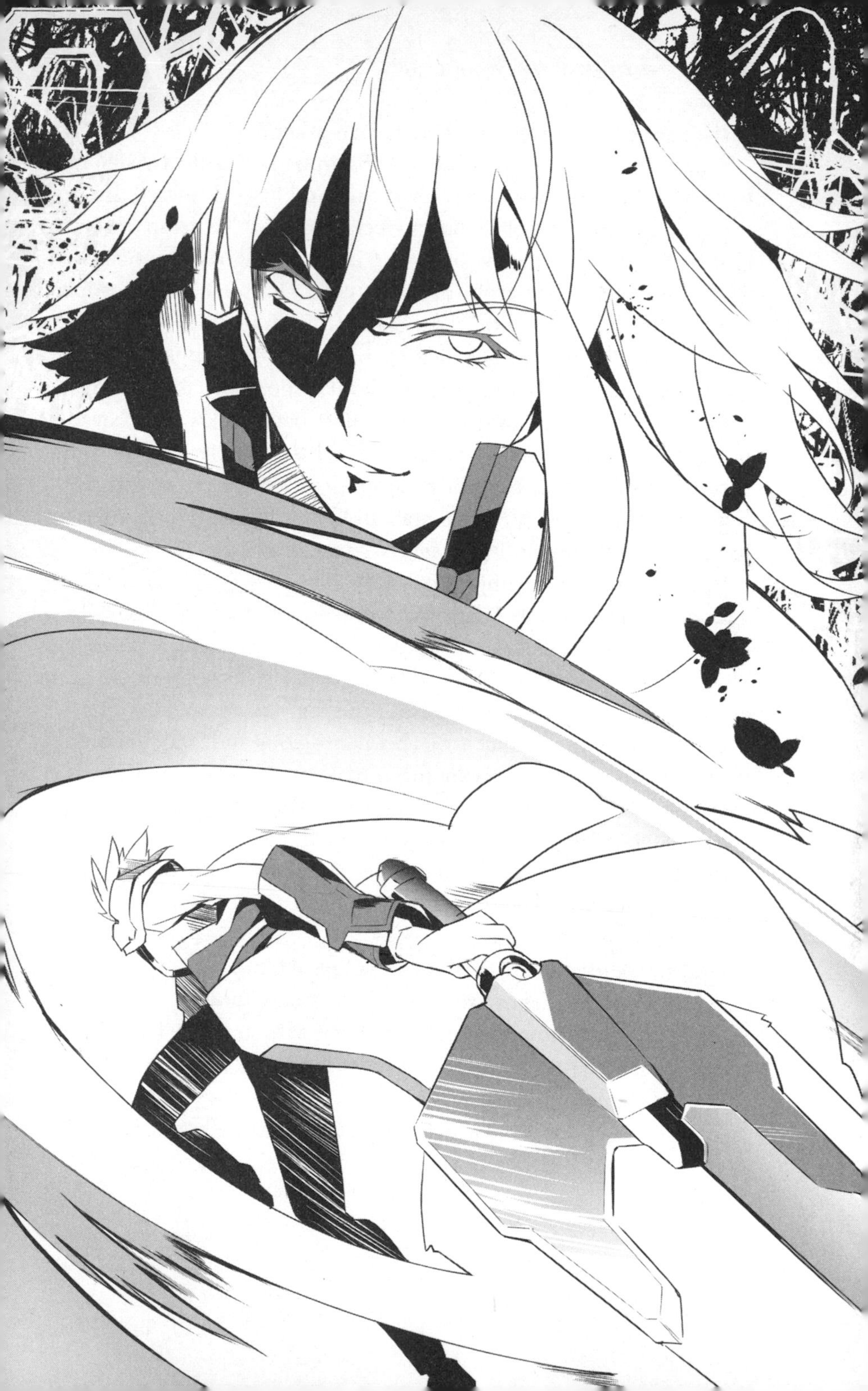

The two roared as they charged at each other.

Ernest, brushing Ayato's downward swing to one side, twisted his body to put himself within reach of him and lunged toward him to trip him up. This kind of grappling technique didn't exist in the Gallardworth style of combat—but it did in the Amagiri Shinmei style. As he approached the ground, Ayato used his free hand to propel himself around to kick Ernest's legs out from under him.

As the Gallardworth boy leaped backward to dodge the blow, Ayato regained his footing and, without a moment's delay, lunged after him with a downward slash. Ernest bent backward to evade it, but the tip of his blade gashed across his chest, tearing straight through his uniform. That didn't stop him, however, from attempting to counter with a powerful stab at Ayato's flank—which, thanks to his quick reflexes, only managed to graze his skin.

Neither was seriously injured.

Even so, at this rate, the two were bound to keep wounding each other, the seriousness of those wounds increasing with every blow. They were both starting to take greater risks with all of their exchanges, both pulling back only at the very last moment.

Ernest's current technique was both ferocious and cold, but being based as it was on his overwhelming mastery of swordsmanship, no matter how rough or unsophisticated it might appear, he was showing no opening that Ayato might take advantage of.

As they continued to exchange blows, their uniforms, Seidoukan and Gallardworth alike, tore with each strike, dashes of blood splashing across the stage.

And yet, neither could deliver a conclusive blow.

What was more, Ernest was always the first to move.

"Ha-ha-ha-ha! How magnificent! How exhilarating! I truly feel alive!" He bared his teeth as he roared with laughter, still not letting up on his assault.

The two locked swords, when all of a sudden, he elbowed Ayato in the chin at point-blank range.

"*Hrk…!*"

Ayato dodged backward out of pure reflex, Ernest swooping down on him yet again. He spat out the lump of blood building in his mouth, preparing this time to be the one to take the offensive.

That way of fighting was the Amagiri Shinmei style's specialty.

"Amagiri Shinmei Style Grappling Technique—*Grindstone Pommel!*"

Ayato moved in on his opponent, diving forward with a diagonal slash from top to bottom. Ernest may have managed to dodge that, but he couldn't escape Ayato slamming the weapon's hilt into his abdomen.

"Guh?!

Ayato didn't stop there, using his free right hand to strike his opponent's chin—only to have Ernest dive his knee deep into the pit of his stomach.

Even having exchanged such fierce blows, both remained armed and ready, neither allowing themselves to sink to the ground in defeat.

As Ernest lashed out with a downward diagonal slash, Ayato met it with an upward strike of his own, both deflecting the other's attack. When they closed the distance, they lashed out at each other with their hands and elbows, homing in on the other's vital organs, just waiting for an opportunity to pin their opponent down.

Blood splattered across the stage with every strike of their blades, punch, and blow, and yet, neither one allowed himself to falter, neither allowed himself to yield so much as an inch of ground.

They were remarkably similar. Ayato was perhaps the fitter of the two, but in terms of raw ferocity, he couldn't keep pace.

Either one might come out of the battle on top.

Even so, if they kept this up, there could only be one outcome. One would end up taking the other's life.

He would have to finish it before it could come to that.

Ayato fought to get his ragged breathing under control as he slowly edged toward his opponent, looking for some kind of opening, anything, when—

"*A halo of mercy and atonement I give to thee,*" came Percival's gentle voice ringing across the stage, followed by a wave of golden light.

Neither Ayato nor Ernest, both fighting at their absolute best, should have had any difficulty evading it.

For both of them, however, this was the perfect opportunity.

The two threw themselves toward each other with all their weight, crashing together with such force that sparks flew in every direction.

A crater erupted at their feet, the force of their blows so strong as to send rubble flying through the air.

They were both putting everything they had left into this close-fought duel.

They each clenched their teeth as they pushed against each other, but the difference in ability was readily apparent. More important than that, however, was that this wasn't a contest of strength, but rather a kind of delicate negotiation.

When finally they pulled back from each other, it was Ayato who retreated ever so slightly.

Ernest only needed a split second to follow through once more.

At that moment, Laetitia's wings of light descended toward him, but Ernest paid that no heed as he lunged toward Ayato's chest with the tip of his blade.

It went without saying that, if Ernest had been his usual self, he would have linked up with Laetitia's wings.

If he had done that, Ayato would have lost then and there.

However…that would have required that he fight as part of a team.

"Burst into bloom—*Anthurium!*"

A shield of fire manifested in front of Ayato's chest, protecting his crest and stopping Ernest's blade in its tracks.

And then—

"*Boom.*"

Six separate beams of Saya's homing blaster made straight for Ernest's own badge.

"Tch!" The Gallardworth student clicked his tongue as he cleared them away with a flick of his blade, but that split-second opening was all Ayato needed.

"Amagiri Shinmei Style, Hidden Technique—*Crescent Carnage!*"

Ayato launched himself off the stage to slice through Ernest's school crest with a rounded arc, when—

"Not yet!"

Just before Ayato's blade could reach him, Ernest managed to block it from making contact.

"Yaaaaaargh!"

Letting out an earsplitting roar, and with a gruesome grin that was a bloodcurdling concoction of savage ecstasy, Ernest pushed back against him.

His longsword glimmered through the air as it sped straight toward him.

With his arms outstretched, Ayato's chest was now vulnerable, leaving him no possibility to defend himself.

And yet—

"Raaaaaah!"

Right.

The Gryps was, first and foremost, a team contest.

"—?!"

Claudia, having jumped out from behind him, parried Ernest's blow with the blade in her right hand while using the chambered one held in her left to home in on his chest.

"Ernest Fairclough—crest broken."

"End of battle! Winners: Team Enfield!"

As the mechanical voice resounded across the now-silent stage, Claudia, the twin blades of the Pan-Dora still gripped in either hand, flashed the fallen team leader an exhausted smile. "As long as I have my companions behind me, even I'm fit to be your opponent, Ernest."

EPILOGUE

"Phew..." When she watched the match finally reach its dramatic conclusion from her hospital bed, Kirin let out a deep sigh of relief.

"At... At last! *The championship is decided! Having risen to the top of this year's two hundred and fifty teams and having snatched glory in the face of their overwhelming numerical disadvantage, it's Team Enfield!*"

"*If this were the Lindvolus, that duel between contestant Amagiri and contestant Fairclough may have ended very differently. That being said, I must confess my surprise that it wasn't Team Lancelot that pulled through here...*"

The excited voices of the announcer and commentator spilled out from the live broadcast projected in the air-window in front of her, along with an indistinct cacophony of cheers and applause.

There could be no mistaking that it had been a severely fought contest.

Kirin's hands, clenched tightly in suspense the whole time, were now covered in sweat. From the moment it started, she had been bracing herself for the worst, unable to relax for so much as a second.

Even now, after having watched Ayato apparently break through his final seal and unleash his true power, and having watched Ernest somehow manage to increase his technique to surpass even that, she still couldn't command her racing heart to calm down.

And while they might have won, she still couldn't bring herself to wipe away the shame that continued to torment her for not having been able to be there herself.

"...Congratulations, everyone," she whispered in a small voice, hands gripping her blanket ever tighter.

She couldn't say she was unhappy. She was, of course, overjoyed to be a member of the victorious team, not to mention immensely proud at having been able to carry the semifinal despite her own paltry ability.

On top of that, even if she was absent from the final match, that didn't mean she wouldn't be able to have her wish granted (although, strictly speaking, that was determined based on how many matches any given contestant had participated in). Now she would finally be able to free her father. That was, after all, her most sincere wish.

And yet, in spite of all that, she still couldn't shake her feelings of shame.

The fact that she hadn't been able to stand beside her friends on the stage, to fight beside them, and to snatch victory alongside them, was, for her, unbearably mortifying.

"I suppose I really am still inexperienced...," she said to the empty room, her shoulders slumping.

She could feel her energy returning to her, albeit it in dribs and drabs, but it was still far from the level at which she could properly control it. Having seen just how powerful Ayato had been during the match, she knew that she still had a long way to go.

Even if only in a minor way, she wanted to be able to stand beside him as his equal.

"Wh-what am I saying...?!"

But just as her thoughts led her into a flustered panic, her mobile began to ring.

She had automatically assumed it must have been from Ayato and the others, but she could see on the air-window that they were all still in the middle of their winners' interview. As she glanced at her mobile, a completely unexpected name stood out.

She hurriedly shut the air-window displaying the live broadcast and opened a new, smaller one to take the call.

As the image of a woman of advanced age appeared in front of her, she all but unthinkingly straightened her back and sat up straight.

"Great-Aunt! I'm sorry I haven't kept in touch…"

*

"Yo, it's been a while," Dirk's low voice echoed through the wide access corridor underneath the Sirius Dome.

On the stage above, everyone would be getting ready for the awards ceremony and the formal closing speeches, so it was all but guaranteed that no one else would come down here.

No one else, that was, except for the person he had expressly summoned.

"What do you want, D? Are you really still hiding behind the name of the institute?" The figure that emerged from the wan darkness belonged to none other than Saint Gallardworth Academy's fifth-ranked fighter, a person who, until just a short time ago, had been fighting as part of Team Lancelot—Percival Gardner.

"It's been what, ten years…? Who would have thought you'd go to Gallardworth of all places? I'll be honest with you—I didn't even realize it myself until I had some people look into it. And you've got the Holy Grail, too?"

"Well, I recognized *you* from the very beginning. You really haven't changed at all. Le Wolfe suits you." Percival continued to look straight ahead, her expression calm and unfazed. "So? You didn't call me here to talk about the past. I've got an awards ceremony to go to."

"Hmph, that goes for me, too." As a student council president, he was, in principle, expected to attend formal events of that kind. "Let's get straight to the point. Come back. Work with me. You'd be much more useful than the dolts I've got now."

"…I don't know what you mean. You want me to transfer to Le Wolfe?"

"Don't be an idiot. You know as well as I do that transferring schools is against the Stella Carta. Don't you?" Dirk clicked his tongue in annoyance as he glared across at her. "Give us...no, give *me* a hand. I'm putting certain plans into motion. If you do that, I'll make sure your wish gets granted."

"...My wish?" At that, her steely expression finally wavered.

"Your wish, yeah. You don't need to take the long way and win at the Festa to get that done. I'll grant it faster than they ever could. And to be honest... I watched the match. You don't have a chance in hell of getting what you want that way."

"...I did the best I could."

"That's what I'm telling you. Your best won't cut it there."

"..."

Seeing that Percival wasn't about to talk back to his abuse, Dirk surmised that she must have also realized that for herself. "You're the one who keeps going on about being a weapon, right? So what you need isn't friends. It's a competent user."

"And that's you?"

"Just think back to ten years ago, and you'll have your answer."

Percival remained silent for a long, drawn-out moment before finally answering. "Very well. I'll hear you out."

*

"Ah... I'm glad that's over. I thought the Phoenix was bad, but now I really am sick of their way of putting fighters up on a pedestal like that." Julis, limping down the corridor as they made their way back to their prep room after the ceremony, wouldn't stop complaining.

"Dear me, and I thought you went straight to the hospital after that one and missed all the formalities," Claudia pointed out with a smile.

"I wish I could have done the same thing this time," Julis retorted before turning her piercing gaze to Ayato. "But one of us is much worse off than I am, and if he wouldn't go, it wasn't like I could, either."

"Ha-ha-ha..." Ayato, his body covered in first-aid dressings, looked away, scratching at his cheek.

To be honest, he, too, had wanted nothing more than to rest, but he couldn't bring himself to turn away the academy's associated publicity groups.

Fortunately, none of his injuries were life-threatening, and with his seal finally being properly unlocked, not even his many wounds could dampen his mood.

"By the way... Are you all right, Saya?" Claudia asked.

"Ah..." Saya, who had been following them all half asleep slowly raised her thumb.

"That's some dexterity you've got there," Julis answered sarcastically, when she suddenly turned tense. "Huh?"

"Hello again, Team Enfield."

Standing across from them, down the corridor, were the various faces of Team Lancelot.

"We didn't have a chance to talk properly up on the podiums. Let me begin by congratulating you all," Ernest said with his usual charming smile. Like Ayato, he, too, was injured all over, his wounds similarly freshly treated.

"...It looks like you're back to normal," Claudia remarked.

"Ah-ha-ha. I feel much better now, thanks to you all. I'd been waiting for an opportunity like this for over ten years... Although, it looks like I've fallen out of this one's good graces," he said, tapping the empty holder at his waist.

The Lei-Glems, it seemed, had turned its back on him.

"You've really put us all in a bind now," Laetitia said, raising her hands to her head. "How could someone with the title of Pendragon, and not to mention the student council president of Saint Gallard-worth Academy, do something like that...?"

Certainly, for someone as supposedly perfect as Ernest to have that level of savagery be exposed so publicly, it was inevitable that he would take a significant hit to his image, not to mention cause a massive headache for the student council.

"That's where the support of the vice president matters most, right?" Claudia broke in. "Everyone's counting on you, Laetitia!"

"What?! Don't start meddling in other people's affairs…! And just so you know, we might have lost as a team, but it was Ernest you defeated this time, not me!"

"…That's rather harsh." Ernest grimaced.

Laetitia, however, didn't even spare him a glance as she thrust a finger toward Claudia. "As far as team combat goes, this just means we've got one win and one loss each! So the real champion is whoever wins the next one!"

"Yes, yes, if you say so… I have a debt to settle with you as well," Claudia responded with a smile.

"I'm the one who was utterly defeated. Ayato Amagiri, that technique of yours is amazing," Lionel said as he gripped his hand firmly in his own.

"N-not at all…"

"Well, it was you, Leo, who got your crest broken." Kevin, standing beside him, grinned. "It wasn't like *I* was beaten or anything."

"You're as modest as ever, I see."

"Come on, Leo. There's no need to take your anger out on me."

Kevin and Lionel all but butted heads as they glowered at each other.

"…It looks like you all get along well," Julis murmured, a touch of surprise in her voice.

"Of course. There's always more than one side to someone."

"I suppose that *is* more persuasive when you say it, Ernest."

"…The same goes for you, too, Claudia," Ayato remarked.

"Well, at any rate, Percival aside, the rest of us are all going to retire from this kind of thing," Ernest said. "I'm glad you were our last match."

"Percival's around your age, so maybe you'll face her again one day. You'd better be ready for it," Laetitia added boastfully, placing a hand on the shoulder of her silent companion.

"…Not at all," Percival replied expressionlessly.

"Well then, I suppose we're going to have a lot of free time from now on. We might have retired, but maybe we'll see one another again one day? In fact, I'll be looking forward to it," Ernest said, calm and invigorated to the last.

With that, Team Lancelot made their departure.

"...There's something dangerous about that one," Saya murmured faintly.

Ayato, who had assumed that she was sleeping on her feet, turned to her in surprise. "Huh? That one? You mean Percival Gardner?"

"Right. She's the only one I couldn't properly gauge."

Saya's tone was unusually grave, but now that she mentioned it, she *was* the one who spent the most time engaging her as an opponent, so if anyone could have made that observation, it was her.

"Come now, we had better make our way to the hospital before worrying about things like that," Claudia said brightly, clapping her hands together as if to change the subject. "Ayato and Julis need proper treatment, and it's about time we reported everything to Kirin properly."

"Ah, right. I'm still a bit worried about her condition," Ayato replied.

"If she sees you like that, she'll be the one who'll worry, though," Julis remarked.

There was no arguing with that.

"Hmm..." Saya sighed. "Well then, let's go. She must be waiting for us," she said, flashing them all a weak smile as if to change the mood.

"At this hour, it will be faster to take the airship, I should think. It won't take long to get ready," Claudia added as she fumbled through her pocket, when all at once, not her own, but Ayato's, mobile began to ring.

As he glanced at the name on the display, his expression suddenly stiffened.

"Huh...? D-Dad?"

AFTERWORD

Hi there, Yuu Miyazaki here.

With this tenth volume, *The Asterisk War* has finally reached double digits! I've got lots of announcements to share with you, but I want to keep the afterword to two pages this time, so I'll be brief!

To begin, with this volume, the second arc of the story, which focused on the Gryps, is complete. It's fully loaded with two full-team battles and probably has the largest cast of any volume so far. The team battles may be over now, but everyone we've come to know from Team Yellow Dragon and Team Lancelot still have roles to play, so their fans can rest easy! Incidentally, my favorite part of writing this one had to be Xinglou's and Xiaohui's backstory.

The eleventh volume will be an episode between acts, so to speak, focusing largely on Kirin. She played an active role this time around, but I can't deny that what happened to her was pretty unfortunate, and I want to make it up to her. Also, I kind of interrupted her scene in the epilogue, along with Ayato's, too—basically, we can expect to hear more from both of them in the next volume!

Now, I know it's late, but the Japanese edition of the eighth volume is going through a reprint. I announced this on Twitter, but it turned out that a certain match was cut from the first edition, which led to some misunderstandings and also made the schedule of the tournament and the total number of matches a little disorienting.

This has been fixed for the second edition. My sincerest apologies for the confusion.

Okiura's beautiful illustrations are once again something to behold! A lot of my favorite characters appear in this one, so if you haven't taken a look yet, I hope you'll enjoy them as much as I do!

Also, don't forget about Ningen's manga adaptation of *The Asterisk War* in *Comic Alive* and Akane Shou's manga adaptation of *The Asterisk War: The Wings of Queenvale* in *Bessatsu Shōnen* magazine! I can't recommend them enough!

And the anime! The first season finished airing last fall, with the second one beginning in the spring, so please be sure to watch it! On top of that, I'm so overjoyed by the positive review of the video game *The Asterisk War: Phoenix Festa*, which came out in March. There's all kinds of merchandise being produced to go along with them, so do take a look!

Lastly, I'd like to thank everyone who helped bring this volume to life.

Once again, I'd like to express my sincerest gratitude to my editor, Mr. I, for standing by me no matter all the difficulties I throw his way. The same goes for Mr. S and everyone else in the editorial department, along with everyone involved in the anime and games, and as always, to you, my readers, I'd like to express my deepest thanks for your continued support.

I'm looking forward to seeing you all next time!

Yuu Miyazaki
February 2016

SEIDOUKAN ACADEMY

SILAS NORMAN

A former companion of Lester's. Attacked Ayato with Allekant's backing but was defeated.

 ## ALLEKANT ACADÉMIE

SHUUMA SAKON

Student council president of Allekant Académie.

ERNESTA KÜHNE

Creator of Ardy and Rimcy.

CAMILLA PARETO

Ernesta's research partner.

ARDY (AR-D)—"ABSOLUTE REFUSAL" DEFENDED MODEL

Autonomous puppet. Fought alongside Rimcy during the Phoenix.

RIMCY (RM-C)—"RUINOUS MIGHT" CANNON MODEL

Autonomous puppet. Fought alongside Ardy during the Phoenix.

HILDA JANE ROWLANDS

One of the greatest geniuses in Allekant's history. Also known as the Great Scholar, Magnum Opus.

NARCISSE PERROY

Vice president of the Ferrovius faction. Architect of the Gran Colosseo.

 ## LE WOLFE BLACK INSTITUTE

DIRK EBERWEIN

Student council president of Le Wolfe Black Institute.

KORONA KASHIMARU

Secretary to Le Wolfe's student council president.

characters

ORPHELIA LANDLUFEN

Two-time champion of the Lindvolus and the most powerful Strega in Asterisk.

IRENE URZAIZ

Priscilla's elder sister. Under Dirk's control. Alias the Vampire Princess, Lamilexia.

PRISCILLA URZAIZ

Irene's younger sister. A regenerative.

WERNHER

A member of Grimalkin's Gold Eyes. Kidnapped Flora.

MORITZ

Appeared in the Phoenix, where he was miserably defeated by Ardy.

GERD

Moritz's tag partner. Defeated by Rimcy.

 # JIE LONG SEVENTH INSTITUTE

XINGLOU FAN

Jie Long's top-ranked fighter and student council president. Alias Immanent Heaven, Ban'yuu Tenra.

XIAOHUI WU

Jie Long's second-ranked fighter and Xinglou Fan's top disciple.

CECILY WONG

Hufeng Zhao's former tag partner, with whom she became a runner-up at the Phoenix.

HUFENG ZHAO

An exceptional martial artist often entrusted with secretarial tasks by Xinglou Fan, who always gives him something to worry about.

SHENYUN LI & SHENHUA LI

Twin brother and sister. Defeated by Ayato and Julis during the Phoenix.

SONG & LUO

Fought against Ayato and Julis in the fifth round of the Phoenix.

ALEMA SEIYNG

Jie Long Seventh Institute's former number one, with overwhelming ability in martial arts.

SAINT GALLARDWORTH ACADEMY

ERNEST FAIRCLOUGH
Gallardworth's top-ranked fighter and student council president.

LAETITIA BLANCHARD
Gallardworth's second-ranked fighter and student council vice president.

PERCIVAL GARDNER
Gallardworth's fifth-ranked fighter and student council secretary.

ELLIOT FORSTER
Fought with Doroteo during the Phoenix, with whom he advanced to the semifinals.

DOROTEO LEMUS
Together with Elliot, defeated by Ayato and Julis during the semifinals of the Phoenix.

 QUEENVALE ACADEMY FOR YOUNG LADIES

SYLVIA LYYNEHEYM
Queenvale's top-ranked fighter, student council president, and popular idol.

MILUŠE
Rusalka's leader. Vocalist and lead guitarist.

PÄIVI
Rusalka's drummer.

MONICA
Rusalka's bassist.

MAHULENA
Rusalka's keyboardist.

TUULIA
Rusalka's rhythm guitarist.

YUZUHI RENJOUJI
Studies the Amagiri Shinmei Style Archery Techniques. Acquainted with Ayato.

characters

VIOLET WEINBERG

Alias the Witch of Demolition, Overliezel.

OTHERS

HARUKA AMAGIRI

Ayato's elder sister. Her whereabouts had been unaccounted for, but she was discovered in a deep sleep.

HELGA LINDWALL

Head of Stjärnagarm.

MADIATH MESA

Chairman of the Festa Executive Committee.

DANILO BERTONI

Former Chairman of the Festa Executive Committee. Died several years ago.

URSULA SVEND

Sylvia's teacher. Her body has been taken over by Varda.

JAN KORBEL

Director of the hospital treating Haruka.

GUSTAVE MALRAUX

One of seventy-seven individuals involved in the Jade Twilight Incident, an act of terrorism.

MICO YANASE

Announcer at the Phoenix.

PHAM THI TRAM

Commentator at the Phoenix.

FLORA KLEMM

A young girl from the orphanage Julis is supporting.

SISTER THERESE

The representative from the orphanage Julis is supporting.

JOLBERT

Julis's elder brother and the king of Lieseltania.

MARIA

Queen of Lieseltania.

SOUICHI SASAMIYA

Saya's father. Lost most of his body in an accident and appears as a hologram.

KAYA SASAMIYA

Saya's mother.

NICHOLAS ENFIELD

Claudia's father.

KOUICHIROU TOUDOU

Kirin's uncle. Planned to use her to boost his career at his integrated enterprise foundation, but failed.

BUJINSAI YABUKI

Eishirou's father, and the head of the Yabuki Clan, aka the Night Emit.

RIKKA: THE ACADEMY CITY ON THE WATER

QUEENVALE ACADEMY FOR YOUNG LADIES

Their school crest is the Idol, a nameless goddess of hope. The culture here is bright and showy, and in addition to fighting ability, another criterion for admission is good looks. It is the smallest of the six schools.

COMMERCIAL
AREA

MAIN STAGE

CENTRAL
DISTRICT

ADMINISTRATIVE
AREA

LE WOLFE BLACK INSTITUTE

Their school crest of Crossed Swords signifies military might. They have a tremendously belligerent school culture that actually encourages their students to duel. Owing to this, their relationship with Gallardworth is strained.

SEIDOUKAN ACADEMY

Their school crest is the Red Lotus, the emblem of an indomitable spirit. The school culture values individuality, and rules are fairly relaxed. Traditionally, they have many Stregas and Dantes among the students.

SAINT GALLARDWORTH ACADEMY

Their school crest is the Ring of Light, symbolizing order. Their rigid culture values discipline and loyalty above all else, and in principle, even duels are forbidden. This puts them on poor terms with Le Wolfe.

OUTER RESIDENTIAL DISTRICT

An academic metropolis, floating atop the North Kanto Mass-Impact Crater Lake. Its overall shape is a regular hexagon, and from each vertex, a school campus protrudes like a bastion. A main avenue runs from each school straight to the center, giving rise to the nickname Asterisk.

This city is the site of the world's largest fighting event, the Festa, and is a major tourist destination.

Although Asterisk is technically a part of Japan, it is governed directly by multiple integrated enterprise foundations and has complete extraterritoriality.

JIE LONG SEVENTH INSTITUTE

Their school crest is the Yellow Dragon, the mightiest of the four gods, signifying sovereignty. Bureaucracy clashes with a laissez-faire attitude, making the school culture rather chaotic. The largest of the six schools, they incorporate a Far Eastern atmosphere into almost everything.

ALLEKANT ACADÉMIE

Their school crest is the Dark Owl, a symbol of wisdom and the messenger of Minerva. Their guiding principle is absolute meritocracy, and students are divided into research and practical classes. They are unparalleled in meteoric engineering technology.

THE WORLD OF *THE ASTERISK WAR* GLOSSARY

THE INVERTIA

A mysterious disaster that befell Earth in the twentieth century. Meteors fell all over the world for three days and three nights, destroying many cities. As a result, the strength of existing nations declined considerably, and a new form of economic power known as "integrated enterprise foundations" took their place.

A previously unknown element called *mana* was extracted from the meteorites, leading to advances in scientific technology as well as a new type of human with extraordinary powers, called Genestella.

The Invertia was undetected by all the observatories in the world, and the destruction it caused was actually much less than ordinary meteors, so the pervading theory is that it did not consist of normal meteors.

INTEGRATED ENTERPRISE FOUNDATION

A new type of economic entity formed by corporations that merged to overcome the choatic economic situation following the Invertia. Their power far surpasses that of the diminished nations.

There used to be eight IEFs, but there are currently six: Galaxy, EP (Elliott-Pound), Jie Long, Solnage, Frauenlob, and W&W (Warren & Warren). They vie for advantage over one another and effectively control the world. Each one sponsors an academy in Asterisk.

THE FESTA

A fighting tournament where students compete, held in Asterisk, and operated by the IEFs. Each cycle, or "season," consists of three events: the tag match (Phoenix) in the summer of the first year, the team battle (Gryps) in the fall of the second year, and the individual match (Lindvolus) in the winter of the third year. Victory is achieved by destroying the opponent's school crest, and the rules are set forth in the Stella Carta. As the event is held for entertainment, acts of deliberate cruelty and attacks intended to cause death or injury can be penalized.

The event is the most popular one in the world, with matches broadcast internationally. The IEFs prioritize economic success and growth above all else, so the direction of the Festa has always been driven by the majority demand of consumers. (This is why the fighters are students—viewers want to see beautiful boys and girls fight one another.) Some speak out against the Festa on ethical grounds, but under the rule of the IEFs, those voices have fallen from justified dissent to unpopular opinion.

The cultures of the different schools veer to extremes, which is also by design, for the sake of the Festa.

THE STELLA CARTA

Rules that apply strictly to all the students of Asterisk. Those who violate these rules are harshly penalized, sometimes by expulsion. If a school is found to have been involved, the administration can also be subject to penalty. The Stella Carta has been amended several times in the past. The most important items are as follows:

- Combat between students of Asterisk is permitted only insofar as the intent is to destroy the other's school crest.
- Each student of Asterisk shall be eligible to participate in the Festa between the ages of 13 and 22, a period spanning ten years.
- Each student of Asterisk shall participate in the Festa no more than three times.

MANA

A previously unknown element that was brought to Earth by the Invertia. By now, it can be found all over the world. It responds to the will of living beings who meet certain criteria, incorporating surrounding elements to form objects and create phenomena.

GENESTELLA

A new type of human being, born after regular human children were exposed to mana. With an aura known as *prana*, they possess physical abilities far beyond those of ordinary humans. Genestella who can tap into mana without special equipment are called Stregas (female) and Dantes (male).

Discrimination against Genestella is a pervasive social problem, and many students come to Asterisk to escape this. (The negative bias against Genestella is one reason why opposition to the Festa is in the minority.)

PRANA

A kind of aura unique to Genestella. Stregas and Dantes deplete prana as they use their powers. They lose consciousness if they run out of prana, but it can simply be replenished with time. The manipulation of prana is a basic skill among Genestella, and by focusing it, they can increase offensive or defensive strength. This is especially effective for defense, which explains why serious injuries among Asterisk students are rare despite the common use of weapons.

METEORIC ENGINEERING

A field of science that studies mana and the meteorites from the Invertia. Many mysteries remain pertaining to mana, but experimentation on manadite has advanced significantly. Fueled by the abundance of rare metals found in the meteorites, manadite research has yielded a large variety of practical applications.

MANADITE

A special ore made of crystallized mana. If stress is applied, it can store or retain specific elemental patterns. Before the Invertia, it did not exist on Earth, and it must be extracted from meteorites. Manadite is used in Lux activators, as well as manufactured products developed through meteoric engineering.

LUX

A type of weapon with a manadite core. Records of elemental patterns are stored in pieces of manadite and re-created using activators. By gathering mana from the surroundings, they can create blades or projectiles of light. Mana also acts as the energy source for Lux weapons.

URM-MANADITE

A name for exceptionally pure manadite, much rarer than ordinary manadite. Luxes using urm-manadite are known as Orga Luxes. Urm-manadite crystals come in myriad colors and shapes, and no two are the same. They are said to have minds of their own.

ORGA LUX

A weapon using urm-manadite as its core. Many of them have special powers, but using them takes a toll—a certain "cost." The weapons themselves have something akin to a sentient will, and unsuitable users cannot even touch the weapon. Suitability is measured by means of a compatibility rating.

Most Orga Luxes are owned by the IEFs and are entrusted to the schools of Asterisk for the purpose of lending them to students with high compatibility ratings.

HAVE YOU BEEN TURNED ON TO LIGHT NOVELS YET?

IN STORES NOW!

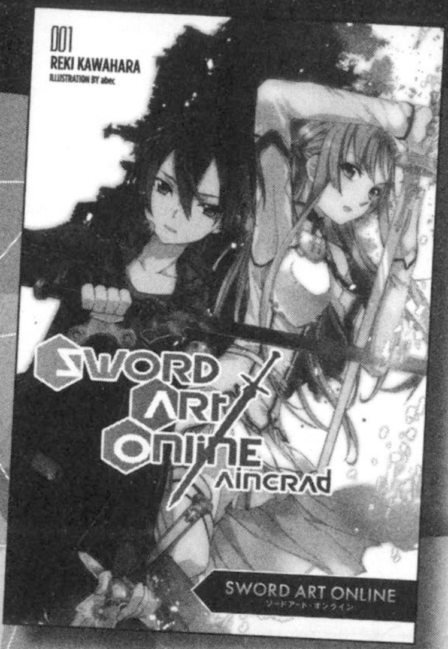
001
REKI KAWAHARA
ILLUSTRATION BY abec
SWORD ART ONLINE
AINCRAD
SWORD ART ONLINE
ソードアート・オンライン

SWORD ART ONLINE, VOL. 1–16
SWORD ART ONLINE, PROGRESSIVE 1–6

The chart-topping light novel series that spawned the explosively popular anime and manga adaptations!

MANGA ADAPTATION AVAILABLE NOW!

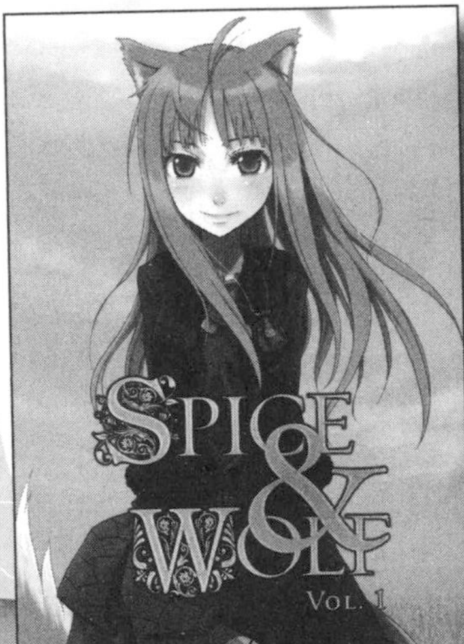
SPICE & WOLF
VOL. 1
ISUNA HASEKURA

ACCEL WORLD, VOL. 1–18

Prepare to accelerate with an action-packed cyber-thriller from the bestselling author of *Sword Art Online*.

MANGA ADAPTATION AVAILABLE NOW!

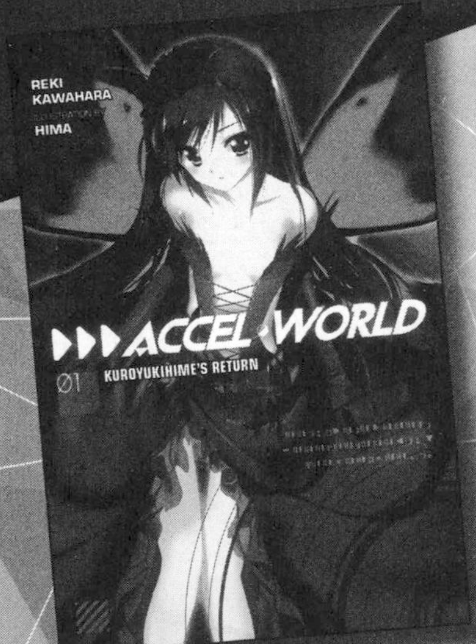
REKI KAWAHARA
HIMA
ACCEL WORLD
01
KUROYUKIHIME'S RETURN

SPICE AND WOLF, VOL. 1–20

A disgruntled goddess joins a traveling merchant in this light novel series that inspired the *New York Times* bestselling manga.

MANGA ADAPTATION AVAILABLE NOW!

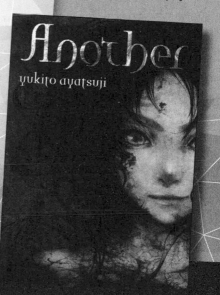